THE MEEK
SHALL INHERIT

by

Gill Cross

Grosvenor House
Publishing Limited

This book is published by
Grosvenor House Publishing Ltd
Link House
140 The Broadway, Tolworth, Surrey, KT6 7HT.
www.grosvenorhousepublishing.co.uk

A CIP record for this book
is available from the British Library

ISBN 978-1-78623-870-2

For Graham

Acknowledgements

Thanks to my lovely multi-talented daughter, who despite working full time manages to paint, write and still find the energy to edit and encourage my fictional works.

Heartfelt thanks also to Dr James Castner in Florida. A prolific author and dear friend, who despite a busy life gathering material in Mexico for his next book, generously gave of his time via emails and such, to proof-read my novel. His reaction to it was a boost indeed.

CHAPTER ONE

An icy wind gathered speed across the meadow, whistling its way through the cracks and crevices of the cottage and leaving a lingering chill inside the meagre dwelling. Through the narrow panes of glass at the window the last glimmer of daylight suddenly disappeared and as Kate crossed the small, darkened room to the fireplace, cold, damp air penetrated the stone floor beneath her feet. She shivered involuntarily and rubbed her hands over her arms to allay the creeping numbness. Then, in a delicate manner, she raised the hem of her rough, linen dress and knelt at the hearth to place a dry log on the fading fire. Her poise and bearing bore a gentility that seemed strangely at odds with the crude surroundings.

She was of medium height and slender build and though the contours of her body were concealed in sombre, grey attire that began at the base of her throat and ended at the projection of sensibly laced shoes, an apron at her midriff gave hint as to the trimness of her waistline. Fine boned features were accentuated by jet black hair, scraped back from the face into a schoolmarmish bun and her deep, brown eyes loomed large with the severity of the style. True her cheeks were pale and lacked that certain lustre befitting youth, but with time and inclination she could have been something of a beauty, for all the ingredients were there.

Now, resting back on her heels juvenile fashion, she stared at the open fire and after a moment's contemplation glanced at the clock on the mantle-piece. A frown wrinkled her brow and returning her gaze to the lifeless bark that sat like an intrusion upon the dying embers, she whispered with urgency, "Burn, please burn." The wood emitted a hiss and crackle and when it finally took hold the darkened room flickered with unaccustomed light. With a sigh of relief Kate eased her body into the nearby rocking chair and as she leaned her head against its hard, wooden struts, her porcelain skin looked ethereal in the fire's glow.

Yet alas, despite comeliness, for all her nineteen years, Kate was a woman deep love had not touched upon. Marriage, a union in which she had sought to be a dutiful wife, kindled nought but humiliation and an aura of desperation hung about her person seeming to add the look of extra years. But, for all that, she was as gentle of voice as was her nature, in truth, the very opposite of her bullying husband whom she had wed but two years earlier.

Jack Pembleton was a huge man, with enormous strength for his fifty years, but there was an ugliness within him that seeped from the very core. Uncouth, unclean and so venomous in his manner toward Kate, his very presence caused her trepidation. That they were a childless couple made her truly thankful, for Jack was given to such fits of evil temper and bouts of heavy drunkenness no child should ever witness. Yet, drunk or sober, his treatment of Kate was the same, less than that of a servant and when it suited, more in keeping with a woman of the streets.

In the nearby village of Hengleford, Kate's name conjured up such imaginativeness one had difficulty in discerning fact from fiction. Yet few had seen her, for she had not set foot outside the boundaries of the farm since her arrival. Indeed the clothes she wore had been purchased by her parents many years before, yet, with perseverance in the art of needle and thread she had become an accomplished seamstress and always took care to be neat of dress. But it was Jack who purchased any household items deemed necessary, allowing no money to pass into his wife's hands.

Tales of the Pembletons spread throughout the close-knit community, mainly from Jack's farm hands, who spoke of rare glimpses into the well-kept cottage, of bruises on Kate's face, or her seemingly painful walk whilst filling up their billycans from the pump outside the kitchen door. Yet none of the womenfolk ever saw fit to visit, for fear Jack Pembleton might stumble upon them.

Outside the wind had dropped and but for the ticking of the clock on the mantle-piece, an eerie stillness pervaded the sparse surroundings of the cottage. The peace was to Kate's liking and a feeling of contentment reigned as she studied the fire's glow and sought to recapture the pleasures of the day. It was Friday, market day and upon her husband's departure in the early morning she had hurried through the household chores and found time for a little self-indulgence. Such times were rare. For awhile she had braved the elements and taken to walking the meadow where the tentacles of the huge oak trees bowed and curtsied under the force of the gusty March winds. The air was fresh, invigorating and with each step of the foot and swing of the arm, the tenseness in her body eased. No longer harassed by Jack's persistent bullying, her mind tempered to the quiet of the morning and she took pleasure in the knowledge that providing all chores were complete, the day was hers, to do with as she wished. Later, nestling in a chair by the warmth of the fire, she turned the pages of a book and was soon transported from her dreary existence into a colourful world of lifelike characters, beset by romance and intrigue.

A strict upbringing had never brought forth a closeness or spontaneous emotion from either of her parents, though in fairness to them both, they had provided her with an education better than most. It was the latter that had instilled her love of the written word and denied as she was throughout childhood the companionship of others, it was left to the magical revelations of literature to fill that void of loneliness. Now she welcomed solitude, indeed, longed for it, as it offered temporary respite from the cruelties inflicted by her husband.

But alas, as is the way of pleasurable moments, the hours sped by and when the clock struck seven, it served as a reminder that soon all would be disrupted by Jack's arrival. Reluctantly, Kate rose from her chair and with fingers twitching nervously at the apron around her waist, reached for a spill and thrust it into the open fire. Slowly at first she lit the oil lamps about the room, then hastily, for fear all would not be ready, moved into the kitchen to make sure the mutton stew prepared earlier was sufficiently re-heated on the range.

Suddenly the clattering approach of pony and trap broke into the stillness of the night. When it came to a halt in the cobbled yard her body trembled at the sound of the noise and furore. Discarding the spill into the roaring fire she hastened to prepare the supper table.

A moment later a flurry of cold night air invaded the cottage and out of the darkness Jack Pembleton appeared, his huge frame reeling back and forth in a drunken stupor. A grubby cap pulled low over his forehead shadowed the ruddiness of bloated cheeks and his rough tweed jacket, stretched to its limits and tied with string about the waistline, bore signs of spillage. He stumbled inside, cursing the night air and with a backward thrust of his heel, kicked the door to a close. Still muttering profanities, he lurched forward to place a bottle of liquor down hard upon the table. As if by avoiding his glare Kate could escape his wrath, she delved into the sideboard cupboard for dishes, though when his lumbering figure moved across the floor behind her, her body trembled in the wake of it, for his mood was a fearful one, already inflamed by a goodly consumption of ale. Presently sensing distance between them, she rose fully and glancing furtively in his direction, watched as he staggered to his chair beside the fire. Freeing himself of his jacket, his bloodshot eyes, bulging with temper, sought hers from across the room.

"Don't just stand there woman," he roared, "help me with me boots."

There was a wildness about him that demanded deference and with a willingness to humour him Kate knelt before him and eased the mud covered boots from his feet.

Jack Pembleton took uncommon pleasure in his wife's servility and as the length and breadth of him warmed to the heat of the fire, a sense of well-being tempered his anger. He muttered not in conversation, merely in thinking aloud. Then his glazed eyes travelled lustfully over the kneeling figure and as he studied the rise and fall of her youthful body, the need to possess her rippled through his loins. With anticipation he edged forward on his seat. A foolish grin distorted his ugly features and as Kate raised her head and saw the look upon his face, a feeling of hopelessness swept over her.

With a suddenness that startled her he pulled her closer, his rough, unshaven chin grazing the tenderness of her own. Her body arched under his tightening grip and as his fingers travelled the line of unhealed wealds across her back, she stifled a cry, knowing full well that a whimper of discomfort could only prolong her agony. She shuddered and as the bristles of his face continued to scrape against her skin, such nausea raged through her body that she made to turn from his whisky soaked breath. Incensed by her revulsion, Jack clutched her chin in a vice-like grip and turned her face to meet his. "Spurn me would yer," he growled, shaking her head from side to side. His cheeks had ballooned into a frightening enormity and powerless to move Kate could only submit to the invasion of his rough, marauding hands.

"Your supper, Jack," she stammered in an effort to placate him. But undeterred by her plea his passion gathered momentum. Impatient now for sight of her, his work soiled fingers tore at the buttons of her dress. Kate crossed her arms to cover her nakedness, but the modesty of her action merely added fuel to her husband's desire. With lightning swiftness he forced her arms apart and with mouth agape and saliva upon his lips paused for a moment to drool at the spectacle. Then, a triumphant gleam swamped his eyes as he discharged a groan of delight.

Kate's back was stiff from its uncomfortable stance and she sorely ached, yet she dare not move, for Jack's leather belt was all too readily accessible and any effort to withdraw from his clutches would find him all too willing to use it. So she remained, obedient, submissive, with her mind beset by the terror of other such occasions. She closed her eyes and prayed that the violation of her body would soon be over. Then, as if in answer to her unspoken plea, as swiftly as her ordeal had begun, so it was over. Prompted by a goodly consumption of liquor, Jack could lust no further. Muttering he had need of his bed he pushed her aside and rising unsteadily to his feet, swayed across the room towards the steep wooden staircase.

Kate watched his faltering, laborious trek and only when the floor boards above creaked under the weight of him as he fell fully clothed upon the huge feather mattress, did relief flood her being. If alcohol had consumed him, then for once she had reason to be grateful and in the stillness that followed, she prepared a bowl of hot water to bathe her aching limbs.

At five thirty the following morning, when Jack Pembleton arose from his bed, such agony began to grip his chest that the need for air to replenish his lungs became a desperate one. The experience of pain was completely foreign to him, indeed, for all his years, despite unhealthy ways, he had never known a day's illness. Now, grey faced and senses reeling, he collapsed heavily onto the floor, catching his head upon the brass bedstead as he did so.

Below, Kate had just put the kettle on the kitchen range when she heard such a commotion from above that she hastened up the stairs, only to find her husband bleeding with much profusion from a head wound, that she wasted no time in calling for help from the bedroom window. Although the hour was early, Ted, one of the younger of the farm hands was already making his way towards the milking shed, but on hearing Kate's cry for help, turned back and hurried into the cottage. Together they lifted Jack's huge frame onto the bed and whilst Kate made an effort to stem the flow of blood with towelling from the kitchen, Ted hurried downstairs and out into the yard to make ready the pony and trap for his journey into the village for the doctor.

It was a bitterly cold March morning, with a hint of snow in the air, nonetheless the elderly Doctor Parkins donned his overcoat and set off eagerly, if only to satisfy his curiosity with regard to the Pembleton household. On arrival, his surprise at the neatness of the cottage was apparent and after tending Jack's wound and giving him a thorough examination, he reflected upon the man's condition as he slowly descended the stairs. Whilst Jack was being attended to, Kate had put a spill to the living room fire, and when the doctor's small, rotund figure suddenly appeared in the doorway she approached him with timidity, for the initial trauma of the moment was now passed and unused to the company of others, shyness overcame her.

"I have some hot water prepared if you wish to wash your hands doctor," she offered quietly.

"That's very thoughtful of you Mrs Pembleton," he replied, waiting patiently whilst she went into the kitchen and later re-appeared carrying a small enamel bowl of hot water, a square of carbolic soap and a clean towel over her arm, all of which she placed upon the table within his reach.

Parkins, by nature a perceptive man, was at once aware of her unease and after washing and drying his hands, he moved across the room to warm his body at the open fire.

"It's a fearful cold wind out there my dear," he remarked, gesticulating towards the window in a friendly fashion.

Kate nodded her head in agreement and with spontaneous politeness offered him tea and the opportunity to be seated. Pleased by the considerate overture Parkins accepted and whilst Kate cleared the bowl from the table and set about her task, his pale, blue eyes observed her fine features and tidy manner and he felt nought but admiration. Indeed, if one was to assume all the tales of her suffering to be true, then he judged her to be a young woman of remarkable inner strength, for many he knew, would have floundered and sunk to a squalid existence.

Presently tea was ready and when Kate seated herself opposite him at the table, he began to speak in hushed tones of the seriousness of her husband's condition. "The head wound will heal with time," he assured her, "though the trauma of it has caused his mind to be somewhat confused. However, I feel this to be a temporary setback. As to the state of his heart, well my dear, this is more serious. To be frank, save for lessening his pain with medication, there is little I or anyone can do to prevent the eventual outcome." He hesitated now and then in conversation to observe the look of concern in Kate's deep brown eyes and mistaking it for affection felt as never before, that he had no understanding of a woman's ways where love and marriage were concerned. But then, in all wisdom, who can know the true manner of any such alliance.

He would have wished to have whiled away more time in her company, for she was, he discovered, a knowledgeable young woman and a conversation had blossomed with regard to a collection of literary works stacked neatly upon the roughly cut shelves set in an alcove by the fireplace. Some were her late mother's Kate confided, but many had belonged to her now deceased father.

At once Parkins was intrigued by what manner of man could have encouraged his daughter's involvement with the likes of Jack Pembleton, but alas, he had little time to pursue the matter, as preparation for a busy surgery that morning prevented further meanders. And so, with instructions as to the dosage of mixture from his bag that Jack was to be given until he returned the following day, he made ready to leave.

The wind had dropped, snow was falling and as Kate stood by the window observing the doctor's departure, a ripple of hope for the future grew within.

Chapter Two

Jack stared vacantly out the bedroom window with unseeing eyes. His illness had provoked an early senility for which there was no cure. Now, subdued and entirely lacking in physical strength, he had become as a child and was content to sit in his armchair. Supported by pillows lest he should slip into the depths of the chair, he posed a pathetic figure of the man he once was. Kate's freedom from his wrath was absolute. That she bore him no malice was tribute only to her gentleness of character, for despite his past cruelty, she could be found feeding him broth and tending to his needs in a caring, maternal fashion. Now, without fear of reprisal, she could at last take satisfaction in her wifely duties.

Her first welcome task was to make the second bedroom in the cottage habitable for her own use. After disposing of all the oddments that had been stored there over the years, she scrubbed and cleaned the area with gusto. Having spoken of her intention to Albert, the elderly farm foreman, he promptly assisted by sending young Ted into the village. The boy returned with distemper and paint brushes and within a short time the area had been transformed into a pleasant, habitable room. An old brass bedstead was found in the barn and polished up like new and when by chance a fresh, flock mattress was publicised in the window of the village store, Albert took the liberty of acquiring and delivering it to Kate's door with the aid of pony and trap.

In the weeks that followed it was necessary Kate should take a more active role in the farm's affairs. There was much to learn, including aspects of breeding. For whilst the property was not the biggest in the county of Northamptonshire, the herd with its fine pedigree had an enviable reputation throughout the shires. A fact Albert took great pride in. But then, he had been foreman at Pembleton farm for many years, and it was he who had steered his employer with regard to purchasing quality stock. Indeed, with Jack's approval he had also offered young Ted work after leaving school. The blond haired, freckle faced youth, now seventeen, had proved his worth time and time again. As for Archie, the strapping fifteen year old who possessed the brightest blue eyes anyone in the village had ever seen, well, he too had become a real asset. He often completed tasks normally done by two men. Whilst neither of the youths cared for Jack Pembleton and had avoided him whenever they could, it would be true to say that they would have walked through fire for Albert. But then, Albert was a kind, diligent man who tended the farm as if it were his own.

Indeed, when Kate approached him on the subject of her eagerness to learn and willingness to help with any task, he set about acquainting her with the basics of cattle farming and problems that could arise. Kate could only marvel at his knowledge and she was especially grateful for his help and advice throughout this difficult period. It was also at this point that she had reason to be grateful for her late father's insistence of meticulous household accounts. Before several weeks had passed she was keeping books with regard to many transactions, the likes of which Jack had never done.

With her husband to nurse and the household duties to attend to, her work load was heavy indeed. But chores were no stranger to her and the welcome release from her former existence far and away made up for their excess. Each hour that passed found her glowing with energy and a sense of accomplishment she had not known before, and she worked with a willingness of one reprieved.

Meeting with others in the village proved her most difficult role and it was with some apprehension that she at first ventured into the happenings of the small community. Nonetheless, when the step was taken, her modest manner at once gained their respect. Indeed, the villagers were charmed by the nature of her shyness and if sympathetic murmurings of her situation assisted in the speed of their approval, relationships were none the worse for it.

So the weeks passed by and after spending many hours in the fresh air, Kate began to acquire a healthy colour to her cheeks and a confidence about her person. And with the tensions of her former life at an end, her body held the promise of a beauteous woman. In truth, Kate mused, if life should continue in this manner she would be more than content.

With the approach of summer, Jack's general health began to deteriorate. His favourite window seat was no longer giving pleasure, for the effort of settling into it proved too exhausting. Even as Kate fed him breakfast, inert mumblings from his feeble frame made it clear that he wished to stay in bed. But the bedroom was pleasant enough, indeed somewhat cheerier than in the past. For with new curtains at the window and a bright patchwork quilt adorning the feather mattress, the accommodation at last showed a semblance of caring. Nonetheless, despite Kate's routine cleanliness, the room bore an aura of sickness that no amount of disinfectant could dispel.

On occasion, Kate paused in her chores to question the cost of her salvation. Her husband's waxen skin was now stretched to a transparent thinness over his skeletal frame and with the loss of much of his thick, grey hair, eyes stared hauntingly from the dark, circled fathoms of their sockets. In truth he appeared a most pitiful sight and the knowledge that his suffering had relinquished her own lay heavy upon her conscience. In a Christian manner she searched her mind for compassion, for in life, there seemed much to bear and so little of it to be understood. At such times as these Kate felt older than her years. With a deep sigh she observed the sleeping figure and closing the door quietly behind her, made her way down the steep, wooden staircase.

Today was market day and there was much to attend to. Albert waited obligingly in the yard, should Kate require assistance with Jack before he left. Once he had satisfied himself that all was well, he made ready for his journey to the market with Archie, who always accompanied him on these excursions. As for young Ted, at present busy with his axe re-stocking the outhouse with ample logs for the copper and kitchen, he too had a demanding timetable. With a number of cattle on their way to market it was an opportunity to give the main cow shed a thorough clean. Meanwhile, Kate busied herself extracting washing from the copper. After rinsing and easing it all through the old, wooden mangle, she proceeded to carry the laden clothes basket outside. There she pegged the items onto a line strung between two wooden posts, across the length of the back garden.

It was almost nine o'clock before she returned to the morning's paperwork upon the table and she had sat down but a moment when she heard a light tapping at the door. Thinking it to be Ted, she called out for him to enter, when in the half open doorway, a distinguished looking gentleman suddenly appeared. His dark handsome features and suit of good quality accentuated the shabbiness of the cottage. "Forgive me," she murmured apologetically, rising from her chair. "I thought you to be one of the hands." The remark was embarrassingly inappropriate and the knowing of it brought a flush of colour to her cheeks.

The hint of a smile crossed the stranger's lips as he spoke. "Mrs. Pembleton?" His voice was deep and bore an air of sophistication.

"Yes," she nodded.

"Would Mr Pembleton be at home?" Removing his hat, he entered further into the cottage.

Kate hesitated, languishing under the newcomer's scrutiny. "Yes, but I..."

"My name is Jameson, Charles Jameson," he stated brusquely, removing his gloves and extending a hand toward her.

The warmth of his grasp seeped through Kate's fingers and in an effort to regain her composure she moved across the room to latch the door behind him. On turning she beckoned him to be seated, noting with admiration the sureness of his movements as he placed a small attache case upon the table. "Well Mr Jameson," she began haltingly, "my husband has been ill for many weeks and is incapable of dealing with business matters. Could I perhaps be of assistance?"

"Then it is impossible to speak with your husband directly?" His deep, blue eyes probed hers as he turned towards her. The room vibrated with his presence and Kate, exposed to his stare, felt weakened by it.

"Quite impossible," she replied softly, "for his speech has been taken by the illness and other than childish mutterings, conversation is of little purpose."

"I am most sorry to hear that." Jameson's dark eyebrows met in a frown.

With a brief nod, Kate acknowledged his sympathetic tone, then, not wishing to dwell upon the matter, hurriedly gathered paperwork from the table and placed it in a neat pile upon the nearby dresser. "Can I offer you some refreshment Mr Jameson? Tea perhaps?" she enquired politely as she turned to face him.

A smile registered in Jameson's deep blue eyes and suddenly the man became a boy. "That would be most kind," he replied, moving aside his attaché case.

Conscious of his gaze upon her, Kate brushed a wisp of hair from her forehead and quickly disappeared into the kitchen. Shortly after, she emerged bearing a large tray laden with her late mother's china and a generous sized tea pot. "Have you travelled far?" she asked, as she began to pour his tea.

"I motored from London yesterday and stayed overnight at the Inn in Hengleford," he replied, eyeing her movements favourably. It was hardly credible he mused, that this lovely creature could be the wife of Jack Pembleton, a vulgar, uncouth fellow as he recalled. Indeed, such doubt had need of confirmation and as Kate placed a sugar bowl and milk jug before him he queried tentatively, "Forgive me, but you are the wife of Jack Pembleton Senior?"

Kate glanced up from the table and nodded her head. "Yes there is no other," she confirmed.

"Quite," he stated in a sober fashion, "if the question should have appeared discourteous I apologise, but you are so unlike I..." his sentence drifted into oblivion and to detract from any unease he made a gesture toward the paperwork upon the dresser. "I see that you are familiar with business matters. Perhaps Mr. Pembleton has mentioned his connection with Jameson and Jameson?"

"No," Kate replied quietly," but then, until my husband's illness I had little book keeping to concern myself with." Such reference to the past brought a flush of colour to her cheeks and afraid of further probing questions, her eyes avoided his as she refilled his tea cup.

Jameson was quick to observe her look of vulnerability and distracted by it sought refuge in his open attaché case. "I see," he continued. "Well what I have here are copies of all the transactions regarding properties purchased by your husband over the last fifteen years." And withdrawing them from the case, he stretched over the table toward her, pointing out relevant details with his finely manicured fingernails.

Kate leaned forward to study the information more closely. As the warmth of his breath drifted across her cheeks, for the first time in her life she found the closeness of another evocative. Indeed, she became so preoccupied by his presence that his words fell upon inattentive ears. When finally he had done, she raised her eyes. "I am afraid I do not understand any of this, Mr. Jameson," she confessed quietly.

"Were you not aware that your husband was, I'm sorry, IS, a very wealthy man?" The look of surprise upon his face matched hers.

Kate's eyebrows met in consternation. "Wealthy?" she gasped, "this cannot be."

Once more Jameson's eyes penetrated hers. "Then perhaps, Mrs. Pembleton," he replied, pausing briefly to scan the pocket book at his side, "I could be of some service to you over the next few days?"

At once his words dispelled Kate's anxiety and she nodded her head gratefully.

"I should best begin however, with an explanation of why I am here today," he continued. "Jameson and Jameson have acted as solicitors and advisors, for many years on your husband's behalf. The manner of business that has brought me here is one concerning certain properties that your husband purchased a long time ago. We understand from the letting agent that excellent prices could be realised at present, should he wish to consider their sale and as he has not been in contact with us of late, a personal visit was found to be necessary. One for which I might add, I am most gratified I was chosen."

Kate noted the innuendo and was flattered by it. Nonetheless, as he spoke further, the extent of her new responsibilities began to dawn and the burden caused her some alarm. "But surely Mr. Jameson," she questioned, "I have no authority to deal with such matters."

Jameson pondered briefly upon her remark and a moment later his voice resumed its confident air. "Not for the present I grant you, but a doctor calls upon your husband with regularity I presume?"

Puzzled by this assumption Kate nodded her head.

"Then I shall make a personal visit to the doctor," he replied, "to obtain all the facts of Mr Pembleton's illness and later acquire proper authorisation for you and my chambers to act on his behalf." Empathy filled his eyes as he directed his gaze upon her. "Please do not worry," he murmured quietly, "I shall see to it that all the necessary tasks are carried out."

Confused by this extra burden Kate nodded her head. "I..." she parted her lips to speak, then, dubious of his reaction, hesitated in her query.

"Go on," Jameson urged, his handsome features creasing into a benevolent smile.

"I am most grateful you are here, for there are certain items of book keeping of which I am unfamiliar. Could I perhaps discuss them with you?"

He looked upon her innocence favourably, his eyes seeming to search the very depths of her soul. "I am honoured you should approach me," he answered softly.

Overawed by the gentleness of his manner, Kate lowered her head lest he should see the admiration in her deep brown eyes.

Two short hours later Charles Jameson made ready to leave. "I shall return the day after tomorrow, Mrs Pembleton. Now please, I beg of you, do not worry. Trust me." He squeezed her hand reassuringly and a moment later departed.

Kate's eyes followed him to the gate and when his automobile chugged out of sight, she closed the cottage door. Exhausted by the morning's development she leaned against it gratefully. To the realisation that her husband was a wealthy man she gave little thought. Her mind was conscious only of the limp, aging dress between her fingers and that he, Charles Jameson should have seen her in so meagre attire. At recollection of her hand in his, a juvenile blush flooded her cheeks. To restore her confidence she made plans to purchase some items of material in the village later that afternoon. Suddenly light of heart and with energies anew, she began to tackle the rest of the chores.

CHAPTER THREE

It was late in the afternoon of the following day when Doctor Parkins arrived at the Pembleton household. The premature birth of a baby had delayed him somewhat, a fact for which he was most apologetic. From the onset of Jack's illness they had become firm friends and in gratitude of this, Kate often prepared a basket of freshly laid eggs for Dora, the doctor's wife. At once Kate could see by his manner that he was overly weary and whilst he ascended the stairs to Jack's bedroom, she set about preparing a fresh pot of tea. Eventually he reappeared and slowly made his way over to the fireside chair, placing his well-worn bag on the floor beside it as he did so. Kate poured his tea and passed it to him.

"Ah, thank you my dear," Doctor Parkins gathered the cup and saucer into his chubby, well-scrubbed hands and sank further into the depths of the fireside chair. "At times such as these, I wonder if early retirement might merit some consideration," he mused.

Kate eased her slender frame on to the seat of the Windsor chair by the table and smiled whimsically in his direction. "An image of you with time to spare is difficult to contemplate."

"Indeed," he replied agreeably. Then, turning his attention to the reason for his visit, said quietly, "You know that Jack has deteriorated rapidly over the past few days Katherine." He watched her face closely for a sign that might help him determine her true feelings. Oh her concern was apparent, of that he had no doubt, but was it possible that Katherine could love this man in a true, wifely fashion. His thoughts bade him speak more openly. "You have never spoken my dear of how you came to meet with Jack. Is it too presumptuous of me to ask?"

A distant look pervaded Kate's eyes and for a brief moment there was an awkward silence. Then, as if she had resigned herself to discuss the subject more openly at some point in the future, she replied calmly, "No dear doctor, in friendship I will tell you. When my schooling came to an end, I kept house for my mother and father. Mother was an invalid you see and of poor health for many years before she died. After her death, father, a man accustomed to habitual care, assumed that as a dutiful daughter I would remain at home and continue as I had done in the past. At that time it was only right and proper I should do so, but when my father died suddenly, I found myself to be completely and utterly alone."

"Had you no other relatives my dear?" enquired the doctor sympathetically.

Kate shook her head.

"Go on." He encouraged, fingering his chequered waistcoat thoughtfully.

"The house in which we lived was a rented one. I had no money to speak of and at the age of almost seventeen found myself without friends or experience of anything other than keeping house," Kate hesitated, for the memory was a painful one. "Then," she continued, "the day after father's funeral, Jack called with regard to rent already overdue on the property in which I lived. I had no work and no means of paying and he made it clear that by the end of that week I would be evicted from the premises. Where would I go? What would I do? I pleaded. The only suggestion he could offer was that I should keep house for him at Pembleton farm."

A look of surprise spread over the doctor's kindly face as he edged forward in his seat. "Do you mean that you are not...?"

Kate silenced him politely with the raising of her hand. "I answered that it would not be fitting or proper for an unattached woman to do so, upon which his immediate reply was, we will wed then."

The doctor shook his head in disbelief. "But Katherine...." He began.

"Oh I could see that his manner was," Kate hesitated, in search of a phrase that would not appear prudish, "something to which I was not accustomed," she continued, "but the prospect of a roof over my head was a great relief." Her eyes misted with recall. "In retrospect," she confided, "I see it as an occasion that you as a doctor must often encounter. My mother and father were all I had in an otherwise lonely world. They were not the most loving of parents, but they held a security that was familiar. At their passing I suffered more anguish than I could ever have imagined. In all my days I have never felt more alone and simply wanted the burden of decision to be taken from me".

"And so my dear, you married Jack Pembleton."

Kate lowered her gaze briefly and nodded.

"And since that time?" he asked cautiously.

Looking up, her deep brown eyes stared directly into his. "That my dear doctor is a question to which in all honesty you would think less of me if I should answer, though I am truly grateful for your concern." She touched his arm in a daughterly fashion and he patted her hand lightly. He understood her meaning and respected her silence. She was indeed a woman any man would have been proud to call his own.

"Well my dear, things will not be easy for you for some time to come. Jack could continue in this way for days, weeks, perhaps months, though I would be doubtful of the latter, one needs a fighting spirit to survive, which oddly enough, considering the man's past, he seems to have lost."

With a sombre look upon her face Kate nodded in agreement.

"My main concern is for your wellbeing. You need a woman's help Katherine," the doctor continued, determined to have his say. "If only that you might have a short break. Why of late, you have rarely stepped into the village and have worked with vigour these many months upon the farm. Would you not let me arrange assistance for you by way of a nurse, so that you might consider a short holiday?"

"That is most thoughtful," Kate smiled, once more moved by his considerate manner. "But where would I go, for I could not travel alone and there is the farm to consider."

"Does the idea not tempt you, even a little?" He smiled persuasively.

"Oh, but it is out of the question at this time," she replied wistfully.

Not to be discouraged Doctor Parkins continued. "Dora has family by the sea you know. She has often promised them a visit. Would you not consider the journey with her? She would enjoy your company and the farm hands are capable of doing their work in your absence. Why old Albert has run things for Jack often in the past."

Kate began to weaken." I give you my word I will consider the possibility."

"Please do Katherine, for the way you are working on the farm and the constant nursing of Jack, sooner or later you will be unable to cope with the strain of it all." The doctor's voice was sombre in the quiet of the room.

"Why I feel wonderfully fit," she exclaimed.

"But of course you do at this moment. For you have recently had a release from all that must have plagued you in the past. No, no, pray let me continue," he insisted, shrugging off her protests. "You are a young woman, whose life has been dominated by others for so long. Now, at last, you have a future in which to be your own self. But if you work too hard in this manner, for too long, out of sheer exhaustion you could become a puppet at the mercy of some new evil."

Kate tilted her head to one side and looked at him quizzically. "Is there not an adage that one learns by one's mistakes?"

"That my dear, is in theory, but in practice it is never so. To be a little reticent perhaps, but still one will plunge foolhardy, remarking this time things will be different. They rarely are you know." Doctor Parkins rose slowly from his chair. "Now Katherine, I really must be off, for Dora will wonder what has become of me."

"Thank you for our conversation." Kate said, lifting the basket of fresh eggs from the table and passing it over to the Doctor's free hand.

"And thank you for placing your confidence in me. And Katherine, do dwell on the matter of which I have spoken. Should you decide upon that holiday I will arrange everything." He moved towards the door then turned to face her. "By the way, a Mr Jameson called to see me regarding the nature of Jack's illness. I gave him all the information necessary. He seemed quite taken by you my dear."

Long after the doctor's departure his words, "He seemed quite taken by you my dear." echoed in Kate's ear. In truth they set her heart a pounding, for that Mr. Jameson's thoughts had lingered upon her sufficient to award comment was indeed gratifying. Later that evening, after changing Jack's bedclothes and giving him some warm milk, she placed the soiled sheets in a large bucket to soak overnight and retired to her bed.

With the early morning light came the steady drumming of rain upon the casement window. As Kate stirred from a restless sleep, in her mind's eye she conjured up a vision of Charles Jameson. His handsome features and deep, blue eyes smiled down upon her. For a moment she lingered in the warmth of her bed, contemplating whimsically the conversation they would share upon his return visit. When eventually she rose to dress it was with extra care, sitting on the edge of her bed before the dressing table mirror, brushing her long black hair with vigour until it shone. On impulse she left it as it fell, with loose waves draped attractively about her shoulders, but, in the doorway of the bedroom, feeling cheap and wanton, she reached for the hairpins so she might arrange it in its usual severe style.

In anticipation of Charles Jameson's visit, she fed and washed Jack early, then busied herself about the cottage, not straying far from it. But in truth, neither heart nor mind shared the physical exercise of the household chores. Instinctively, at the sound of footsteps she found herself drawn to the window, hoping for a glimpse of him making his way through the gated entrance of the farm. Eventually, through a curtain of rain the sun appeared and the day became dry and sticky with the heat. The meadow looked particularly inviting and though Kate longed to walk amongst the grazing cattle, she dare not leave the oppressive heat of the cottage for obvious reasons.

The hours passed slowly and as Kate paused between chores to reflect upon Mr Jameson and their first encounter, she chided herself for behaving in such an immature manner. He seemed an honourable man and would surely have shown such courtesy to any woman in her predicament. Why, oh why, when life had begun to hold order and contentment, had this stranger stepped into it and thrown her physical being into turmoil.

To contain her meanderings she busied herself with a batch of baking, but alas, when all her tasks had been exhausted and daylight ended with the suddenness of only a very hot summer day, disappointment flooded her soul. With a pang of anger directed towards Charles Jameson and a tetchiness with herself, she closed the curtains, lit the oil lamps and made her way up to her husband's bedroom, to settle him for the night.

On descending the stairs with an empty water jug, she heard a gentle tapping on the door of the cottage and her heart skipped a beat. Cautiously she opened the door and with joyous relief found Charles Jameson standing there. All anger behind her now she beckoned him to enter.

"I realise that it is very late" he murmured apologetically, raising his hat in a gentlemanly fashion.

"No matter," Kate responded calmly, "do come in."

He nodded his head in gratitude as he stepped further into the room. Kate closed the door behind him and hoped with all her being that he could not hear the thunderous noise of her heartbeat.

"Forgive my calling at this hour," he continued, turning towards her, "I wanted simply to reassure you that I have set the wheels in motion with regard to your husband's affairs."

Even as he spoke Kate knew full well that the information would have lost nothing by its keeping until the morning. Nonetheless, his words dispelled any doubts she had endured throughout the day and her mind wallowed in a warm glow of satisfaction. "It is most kind of you to call when you must be weary with so much travelling." Her deep brown eyes scrutinized his. "Would you care for some refreshment?" They were but two steps apart in the stillness of the ill lit room, neither moving, but suspended as puppets on a string of hesitation.

"Mrs Pembleton, Katherine." He spoke her name with tenderness. "I may call you Katherine? I must confess I was most anxious to see you again." His inert body awaited her reaction.

Kate studied his features openly, her fingers aching to smooth his furrowed brow. "And I was most desperate to see your face once more." Her voice was husky with emotion.

Moving swiftly towards her, Jameson took her hands into his own and raised them to his lips. "My dear, I have looked forward to our meeting with such trepidation you cannot know." He whispered.

Kate trembled in disbelief. Could this really be happening? The moment was beyond her wildest fantasy and quivering under his spell she lost all power to move.

"Katherine, my beautiful Katherine, I have thought of little else but you since our meeting. I am truly bewitched." Jameson's handsome features looked down upon her. "Dare I but hope that there is some feeling in your heart for me?"

Kate's eyes, wide with innocence, searched his own. "Can you not see the answer," she stated with childlike honesty.

With a swiftness that took her breath away, his arms encompassed her and as the fullness of his lips searched and found her own, her body began to tremble to the strains of unfamiliar ecstasy. His presence consumed her and to Kate, nothing could compare to such elation. In truth, it would seem that for all the lonely, loveless years, here at last was a kindred spirit to satisfy her innermost yearnings and with all the tenderness and passion allied to love, she returned his fervour. Steam from the kettle she had placed on the range earlier, hung like a thick damp mist about the room and radiant in her acquiescence, Kate freed herself from his arms, hurried into the kitchen and moved the tea kettle to a cooler position upon the grid. At once Charles was behind her, pressing his lips against her hair and when his arms closed around the pounding engine of her racing heart, she leaned back against him gratefully.

Presently she turned to face him, her eyes misty with need. "After so short an acquaintance is it really possible?" she asked quietly.

"Is what really possible my dearest?" Charles murmured patiently in her ear.

"I love you," she said, in awe of the realisation that never before had she spoken the words.

"And I love you," he reiterated, the words coming readily from his lips. Suddenly, the clock in the living room chimed ten-thirty. "I must go," Charles whispered, releasing her from his embrace, "for things would not go well for you if your friends in the village were aware of my late visit."

Kate nodded her head in understanding, not wishing him to go, but grateful for his respect in doing so.

"I shall return tomorrow at an hour more befitting," he said, turning to leave.

"What will become of us?" Kate queried sadly.

He kissed her lips to hush them. "Tomorrow, we will speak of this tomorrow."

A moment later he was gone and as Kate bolted the door, her face was flushed with unfulfilled desire. Later, in the darkness of her bedroom, the previous hour seemed but a magical fantasy. Indeed, as she tossed and turned the night away, endless questions filled her mind and when she finally drifted into a deep exhausted sleep, still they remained unanswered.

The following morning, in anticipation of what the new day would bring forth, Kate arose and dressed especially early. Eager to walk the meadow before the sticky heat of day, she assured herself that Jack was sleeping peacefully and made her way quietly down the steep wooden stairway.

Once out in the fresh dewy air, her body relaxed and tempered to the solitude of the morning and as she gazed at the rambling hills surrounding the farm and the oak trees that stood tall and erect against the pale, blue skyline, the splendour and majesty of it all brought a lump to her throat. Is it that one who sees with the eyes of love can be so much more aware than other mortals?

Resting her back against a nearby tree she felt the ruggedness of its bark through her summer attire. If only Charles could be with her to share the moment she pondered thoughtfully, as she turned to trace the ridges of wood with her slender, work worn fingers. It was but five of the clock, when the sound of a motor vehicle on the approach road to the farm startled Kate from her reverie. For fear of the noise disturbing her husband, she rushed to the nearby fence to halt whoever it was coming down the lane. It was Charles and at sight of him her heart began to race.

He saw her at once and switching off the engine alighted from his automobile and made his way toward her. "Katherine, what are you doing out so early? Is something wrong, could you not sleep my dear?" he asked with touching concern.

Her face glowed with unexpected pleasure at their meeting. "That same question had occurred to me with regard to your good self," she replied with an air of confidence.

"I came to place this letter under your door," he remarked, extracting an envelope from his pocket and handing it to her. "It is unfortunate, but I have to go back to London. An urgent message was awaiting me on my return to the Inn yesterday." Kate's face clouded with disappointment. "It is for a few days only Katherine, hopefully I should return early next week." And with a disarming smile he took her by the hand and led her towards the wooded area beside the meadow.

"I was thinking of you but a moment ago," she confessed quietly, "wishing that you could be here."

A playful expression illuminated Jameson's deep, blue eyes. "Ah, you see, even at a distance I am yours to command," he replied light heartedly, squeezing her hand.

Nonetheless Kate remained perplexed by the news of his imminent departure and seeking reassurance she studied his features in earnest. "You, you will return?" she urged, as her feelings oscillated between confidence and doubt. Then, embarrassed, as such words did not come easily, she averted his gaze.

"Of that there can be no doubt my dearest one," he answered softly, drawing her towards him and brushing his lips against her own. Instinctively Kate's arms began to close about his neck and at once Jameson released himself from her embrace. "This is most careless of me Katherine, for we may be seen, and I want no ill will to harm your sweet self," he remarked cautiously.

"But no one is expected hereabouts until five-thirty," she said and at once her face coloured at the brazenness of her statement. What was happening to her that she should behave so, her conscience questioned.

Charles feigned a look of horror. "Is it possible that this bewitching creature is the serpent of temptation from the very garden of paradise." He laughed and bending towards her, kissed her fully upon the lips. "Very well," he continued, "I shall stay but a moment, and then be on my way to London."

Hand in hand they walked into the depths of the wood and when beneath the sheltering trees, sight of them was lost from the roadside, Charles gathered her into his arms. It was then Kate knew that the evening before had been no childish fantasy, for his touch aroused such uncontrollable longing within her, that the very trees above seemed to be spinning and moving. Soon the meeting of their lips added and multiplied and as desire was about to encompass them, the church clock from the nearby village chimed five-thirty. The sound of it forced Kate back to reality and she pulled away from Charles's ardent embrace.

"What is wrong Katherine?" he questioned, his face flushed with desire.

"You must go Charles," she said, fastening the buttons of her dress with trembling fingers, "Ted will be arriving at any moment."

Reluctantly, Charles agreed, and though irritated by her rapid withdrawal could see the wisdom of her words. With a swift kiss and promise to return as soon as he could, he bade her farewell and hurried over the meadow towards his motor vehicle. Anxious to install herself in the kitchen before Albert arrived, Kate made haste back to the farmhouse. She had no sooner climbed the wooden staircase to ensure that Jack was still sleeping, when there was a knock at the door.

Hurrying down to open it, she found Ted, cap in hand standing there. "Sorry to trouble you Mrs P," he began, "but I've got a message from a gent who passed me in the lane in his motor. He said I was to make sure you found a letter he'd shoved under your door earlier. He didn't like to knock in case he disturbed you."

Fortunately Kate had placed the opened letter on the table after returning to the cottage. Now it shocked her to think how devious she was becoming. "Oh thank you Ted, that would be Mr Jameson," she said quickly pointing to the envelope, "he was due to look over some official documents later today, but on reading this I understand that he has been summoned back to London."

"Nothing up is there?" the lad's eyebrows knitted together in a look of concern.

"Oh no Ted," she answered with a smile of reassurance, "it's regarding paperwork to do with the farm. Would you like a cup of tea before you start the milking?"

"Thank you all the same but I'd best get on with things before Albert gets here," he replied and with a nod of his head, he replaced his cap and a moment later was striding across the yard towards the cow sheds.

CHAPTER FOUR

An hour after leaving Pembleton farm Charles Jameson was well on his way to his chambers in London. Though the journey was proving an uneventful one, it did allow him in part to reflect upon the pleasures given by Katherine Pembleton. In truth he had been quite taken by her from their first meeting. Nonetheless, he was somewhat surprised, indeed alarmed, that she should have been so readily submissive. He had expected a little more reticence with regard to his advances, thereby making the seduction a more exhilarating challenge. But alas, to this date, he had found the female species, regardless of class, all too easy victims and whilst his ego was recompensed, his mind was not. Indeed, what had begun so exciting a prospect, now, for him lacked further interest and other than simple curiosity as to how such a beauty ever came to marry Jack Pembleton, he had no wish to dwell further upon the matter. Upon return to chambers he would approach his elder brother Edwin and suggest that he might deal with any further business on old Pembleton's behalf.

After two stops en route, one for fuel and the other to visit a valued client, his thoughts suddenly turned to those of an early lunch, as there was an emptiness in his stomach that growled noisily for replenishment. On nearing the outskirts of the City he spied the Nelson Inn, a favourite eating place that by chance had a most delightful serving wench and parking his automobile in the cobbled yard, he promptly dismissed the Pembleton case from his mind.

That Charles should have acted in the manner he had, would have been of little surprise to Edwin his brother, or indeed many of the wealthy women of their acquaintance. For Charles Jameson, still a bachelor at the age of thirty-two, represented a handsome figure about the city, both in stature and in features. At well over six feet in height, with a muscular fitness that would have put an accomplished athlete to shame, his dark good looks, accompanied by an easy charm and sympathetic nature, made him an undeniably attractive companion and amour for all women that crossed his path. This belied in time his true character, which was both fickle in heart and mind, for he found little pleasure in routine and moved skilfully and successfully from one relationship to another. Those who could see through this façade were only too flattered by his attentiveness whilst it lasted, but alas, others of inexperience, revelled in his advances, claiming theirs the heart that had won his own, only to be left distraught when, for Charles, the charisma was at an end.

He had the bearings of respectability and the behaviour of a stud. In between were many endearing qualities that made most women more aware for having known him.

It was almost half past three when Charles finally entered his brother's chambers. "Good afternoon Edwin." he remarked cheerfully, striding with ease over the thick, heavily patterned carpet.

Edwin, engrossed in paperwork, ignored him as he perched happily upon the corner of the huge oak desk, but as Charles proceeded to browse through the documents at his side, he snatched them from his hand, his grey eyes cold with anger. "So, you have finally decided to return. You received my message I trust?" he queried, raising his head.

"Mm...." Charles nodded his head.

"Then what in God's name kept you?" Edwin retorted. A look of displeasure crossed his strong angular features as he waved his hand to silence Charles's explanation. "No, do not trouble me with the details. You knew of your morning's appointments of course."

Charles's eyes twinkled impishly. "Nothing that the capable Miss Bartholomew and your good self could not cope with I suspect."

"We coped admirably, but that is not the point Charles. You should have been here. That is what you get a more than adequate salary for." Edwin's voice was tinged with sarcasm.

"Tut, tut Edwin," Charles said, springing to his feet, "I'll come back later when your mood is more receptive."

Ignoring the remark Edwin continued, "Well, what of your farmer friend Pember...?"

"Pembleton," Charles corrected, knowing this was not the moment to suggest Edwin's intervention of the matter.

"Well," Edwin goaded impatiently, "you have dealt with it have you not?"

"It is not as straightforward as we had imagined," Charles replied, moving from the desk to adjust his tie before the large, gilt mirror hanging on the wall.

"What of the sale of the properties in question?" Edwin persisted, anxious to get to the point.

Charles's handsome features bore a sympathetic frown as he turned to face his brother. "The position is this Edwin, the man is very ill, so ill in fact that his wife is having to…"

"Confound it," Edwin exploded, "whenever you are delayed there is certain to be a woman involved." He hesitated briefly, then his lips curled with a smugness unbecoming, "but surely Pembleton's wife is a little below your station."

Charles's face reddened. "It is impossible to speak further if you continue to take such an attitude," he said in a hurt tone.

Edwin waved him on impatiently. "Go on – go on."

"As the woman was so besieged by paperwork, I offered my assistance. With respect, should more business come our way from this affair, it is wise is it not, to see that records are kept in an accurate business-like fashion. I also acquired information from the local doctor with view to obtaining power of attorney for Mrs Pembleton and our chambers to act on her husband's behalf."

Edwin's face twisted with anger. "Are you telling me that you have been away for days and that the sum total of your achievements is the satisfaction of assisting Mrs Pembleton with her book work and making a visit to the local doctor?"

"You know full well Edwin that these matters are time consuming," Charles insisted, "why the poor woman was quite taken aback to receive the knowledge that her husband is a wealthy man. They live in such squalid conditions."

"No more," Edwin cried, gesticulating with frustration, "I cannot bear such tales of woe. But what of your next action?"

THE MEEK SHALL INHERIT

"There," Charles emphasised, "is a problem indeed, for I have to visit Chingwell Hall next week. The Parbury's have invited me to discuss their immediate financial dilemma and this will allow no time at all to deal with the Pembleton situation. Perhaps you could read over the details and handle it for me for the time being." Charles breathed a sigh of relief. There, it was out.

"You humbug Charles, I know you only too well. YOU I suspect, wish me to take over the Pembleton case completely do you not?" Edwin shouted.

"It is impossible for me to be in two places at one time Edwin and should it be necessary an excursion into the country might greatly benefit your health." Knowing he was to have his way Charles released a smile of satisfaction as he moved towards the door, "and now I must leave you dear brother," he remarked cheerfully, "as I have an appointment with the Shepperton's at four. Au revoir."

He closed the door quietly behind him and Edwin knew full well that to argue further would have made very little difference. The Parbury's were influential people and Charles in his usual manner had the elderly Mrs Parbury in the palm of his hand. With a sigh of resignation Edwin placed his finger over the button on his desk and a moment later, the sombre figure of Miss Bartholomew entered the room.

"Yes Mr Edwin." She queried, lowering her chin and staring at him over the top of her metal rimmed spectacles.

"Would you get me the Pembleton file from Mr Charles's office please," he asked, looking up at her briefly, "and you may bring tea through now."

"Yes Mr Edwin."

As a matter of urgency, by the end of the following week, notification for Kate Pembleton and the solicitors to act on her husband's behalf was received at the chambers of Jameson and Jameson, whereupon a letter was sent post-haste to advise her that someone would be calling shortly to discuss the subject further.

From the moment Kate received the communication of Charles' impending arrival her body tingled with a great expectation. Almost two weeks had passed without word or sign since their early morning rendezvous. During that time, she had been troubled by her own naivety and worried lest in retrospect Charles should think badly of her. Would he understand her behaviour? Would he be vexed by her eagerness to succumb to his advances? On return to London had he, a true gentleman, found himself suspicious of her enthusiasm to please after all he knew nothing of her past. Her mind had been in turmoil and physically she had little desire for food. Indeed, only two days before, Doctor Parkins had remarked upon her health and insisted that she thought over carefully the offer he had made with regard to a holiday.

Then the letter had arrived and though it had been brief and impersonal, and not as she would have wished by Charles' own hand, the message dispelled her fears. After what seemed an eternity he would at last be visiting her and all would be well. With renewed enthusiasm Kate set about the task of preparing a dress for the occasion.

It had been many years since Edwin Jameson had found the time or inclination to leave London. Indeed he preferred to remain within the confines of his bachelor apartment or chambers in the city where he felt most at ease. The social side of business affairs was left to his brother. It was an area of the profession Charles eagerly accepted and though Edwin was aware of the numerous escapades in which he indulged, as long as it did not interfere with the smooth running of the company, it was a situation he chose to ignore.

There were but two years between them, yet as brothers they were worlds apart, for whilst Charles was gregarious by nature and most at ease in the company of others, Edwin was an intellectual, favouring hobbies more suited to his enquiring mind, such as the endless shelves of books in his possession, and a valuable collection of art. It was a veritable hoard, rarely seen by others as Edwin discouraged visitors to his rooms and though he did not profess to be an authority on the subject, the paintings he chose to purchase would often prove to become much sought after and to have grown considerably in value.

Edwin, a private man, did not shun people to the point of rudeness but he was always happy to retreat from visitors as soon as the opportunity presented itself. If ambitions were to be had on his part there was but one, to paint with the clarity of the masters that hung about his walls, but in truth, no one knew of this longing. It was a secret he had held for a number of years and though on occasion his daily help Mrs Kemp cleaned and tidied the small attic room filled with materials that would have enthralled any reputable artist, her awareness of his own attributes went no further than the door.

Today, as he motored from the noise of the city, the tenseness in Edwin's body eased and with surprising swiftness he began to relax in his venture of the quiet country lanes. Indeed, such was his enjoyment that he lingered en route to partake of food at a pleasant wayside Inn and it was almost two o'clock in the afternoon by the time he reached Pembleton Farm.

Meanwhile, Kate, clad in a lengthy cotton dress of pastel blue check that she had just completed, made herself ready for the joyous reunion and at the sound of an approaching motor vehicle rushed to the door, only to hesitate momentarily behind it lest she should appear too eager. Eventually she emerged and at sight of Edwin her eyebrows arched in surprise.

"Mrs Pembleton?" Edwin queried, alighting from the car and raising his chequered cap politely, "I am from Jameson and Jameson solicitors." And moving towards her he took Kate's limp hand into his own.

"Charles, Mr Jameson, is he not with you?" Kate prompted, trying desperately to hide her disappointment.

"Er, no," Edwin replied cautiously, "but I…"

Embarrassed now by her lack of discretion, Kate quickly gathered her senses "Forgive my rudeness," she interrupted, opening the door wide, "please do come inside."

Edwin lowered his head as he stepped over the threshold and once inside the cottage stood gazing leisurely about the room. With Albert's assistance Kate had done much to brighten its appearance and the walls now bore a fresh coat of delicate green distemper. Bright flowery curtains graced the windows and though the place remained sparse and lacking in many of the basic comforts, the effort had been made and was pleasurable to the eye.

"You have had a long journey. I'll get some refreshment," Kate continued, indicating a chair," please be seated."

Edwin's grey eyes followed her movements with interest as she prepared the tea. Her hair was neat, with the habitual bun held by pins to keep it firmly in its place. On many the style would have appeared staid, matronly even he surmised, but it heightened the petite profile of her nose and accentuated a maiden-like innocence that proved quite disarming. Indeed, she was a most stunning woman, much younger than he had assumed, unwise in the ways of those such as Charles I'll be bound, he reflected.

It was clear to see she had thought Charles to be arriving and he would have been a fool not to notice the disappointment clearly shown upon her face. "Mr Charles could not fulfil his engagement with you at the very last moment," he said loudly. "It was indeed unfortunate that he was summoned elsewhere, but he asked me to extend his apologies." Goodness knows what prompted this lie, but Edwin felt better for the saying of it. The explanation proved sufficient to remove Kate's crestfallen look and her face relaxed into an engaging smile as she poured his tea.

"I understand," she replied softly, placing a cup and saucer on the table in front of him.

Edwin reached for it gratefully and as he did so glimpsed a set of neatly stacked books upon the shelves. "Ah, you read the classics I see," he said rising from his chair to examine them more closely.

"Yes many times, I treasure them dearly." Kate looked up from the table, paying him more heed.

"All are well worth the reading more than once. One never fails to discover something missed on a previous study, don't you agree?" Edwin remarked, turning to face her.

She nodded her head in agreement. "You read also for pleasure Mr?.."

"Forgive me, Edwin, Edwin Jameson. Charles is my brother. Yes indeed, first out of necessity, but secondly, I believe it is one of the finer ways in which to relax at the end of a weary day."

Kate studied his features. "It would be most difficult to define that you and Mr. Charles are brothers," she concluded innocently.

Edwin was flattered by her interest and felt no discomfort. "My brother and I differ in many ways Mrs Pembleton," he confirmed with an appealing smile.

Whereupon Kate wondered apprehensively how much Charles had confided in his brother of their first encounter. There was a moments silence as she collected her thoughts.

"How is Mr Pembleton?" Edwin continued courteously.

"He worsens daily," she replied quietly, seating herself in the chair opposite.

"Is there no hope whatsoever for a complete recovery?" his grey eyes looked at her directly.

"None," she uttered calmly, "it is simply a matter of time."

Her composure was to be admired Edwin mused and the tone of resignation in her voice forestalled sympathetic murmurings on his part. They would, after all, have served no purpose and appear but a futile gesture. Nonetheless, Edwin understood now why Charles had been so eager to assist her in her troubles for he too found himself deeply moved by her situation. "Perhaps there is some way in which I can be of help to you in my brother's absence, though your book work is up to date I understand."

"Thank you, but there is nothing," Kate stated, raising her hand to shield her eyes from the beam of sunlight that had suddenly appeared through the window.

"You are most fortunate to live in such an area Mrs Pembleton, the Northamptonshire landscape is quite beautiful," Edwin began. Suddenly a thought struck him and he acted upon it.

"I am hoping to see more of the countryside whilst I am here, so I have booked a room at the 'Coach and Horses'. I wonder, is there anything I can purchase for you in the village, or better still, perhaps you could accompany me?" he remarked hopefully.

Still smarting from the non-appearance of Charles, Kate's brown eyes flared with unaccustomed anger. "I have little time to spare for joy riding Mr. Jameson," she replied, more sharply than intended.

Edwin recoiled at her tone. "Forgive my ignorance of your situation," he said, promptly opening his attaché case and removing papers from it. "I will delay you as little as possible."

At once Kate regretted her brusqueness. "No please," she insisted hurriedly holding up her hand, "forgive my manner, but the morning has been fraught with problems. In truth I would welcome a breath of air and it is most kind of you to make the offer. Indeed there are items I require in the village." Even as she spoke, she moved outside to make arrangements for Archie to keep vigil in the cottage whilst she was away. A moment later she re-entered the room and looked at Edwin directly, "I have not had the pleasure of a motor car journey before Mr Jameson and the experience will be quite new to me." She remarked happily.

"In that case may I be permitted to take you for a short drive after business in the village is completed?" he offered jovially, excited at the prospect of her company for a longer period.

"We shall see Mr Jameson," she answered cautiously as she reached for her bonnet hanging on a wall hook behind the door. At once Edwin rose from his chair and after placing several documents upon the table for her signature later, he promptly held the front door open wide and escorted her to his automobile.

With the hood fully down on the Lanchester motor vehicle they were able to take full advantage of the hot, July afternoon, and as the sun shone from an azure blue sky, Kate was happy to have abandoned, if only for a short period, the numerous chores of the day. The countryside was rife with colour and with boyish enthusiasm Edwin glanced appreciatively from side to side in awe of it. "Ah, if only one could capture this magnificence on canvas," he said aloud, emphasising all around him with the wave of his hand.

"To create a painting of such beauty would indeed be a worthy enterprise," Kate replied agreeably, warming to his exuberance.

"You savour good paintings then Mrs Pembleton?" he enquired eagerly, glancing in her direction.

"I have seen but few," Kate sighed, "though the pleasure has stayed ever with me."

"I have a modest collection of my own," Edwin confessed eagerly, "Perhaps you would permit me to show them to you should you visit the city?" Surprised by his own remark Edwin found she was affecting him in a most delightful way.

"I would doubt the necessity to make such a journey, but in the event that I should, I would be most happy to see your treasures," she concluded encouragingly.

"I hope that you will not keep me too long awaiting the privilege," he replied, himself an excited scholar at the prospect.

Soon they entered the community of Hengleford, passing a row of tiny, thatched cottages complete with window boxes that displayed a kaleidoscope of colour. Beyond the square, to the left, was the village store, where outside the premises, a wooden stand exhibited fresh fruit and vegetables, all protected by a dark green and white striped canopy hanging from above. Ahead, to the right, was the 'Coach and Horses' a sixteenth century building, constructed of sandstone and thatch and most pleasing to the eye. In the tranquillity of the afternoon, sprawled lazily on the doorstep, was Landlord Simm's golden spaniel, soaking up the sun.

"Your doctor – Doctor Parkins, is his house quite near?" Edwin asked as they approached the village store.

"There is a narrow road that runs by the side of the Inn; the doctor's detached house is at the end of that lane. It is not very far." Kate pointed.

"Ah, then I shall visit him whilst you attend to your chores," he stated, bringing the car to as gentle a halt as the machine would allow. After assisting her from the vehicle, he tipped his forelock in a chivalrous manner and carrying his attaché case in his left hand, began to stroll leisurely towards the doctor's abode.

Kate's eyes followed him as he walked the length of the road. He was not strikingly handsome, but there was an attractive quality about his sober features and polite manner that was most appealing. Indeed, he was a stimulating companion and once more she regretted her attitude towards him earlier. A moment later she crossed the threshold of the store to a pleasant tinkling of bells, whereupon the cheerful smile of its owner, Emily Potts, suddenly appeared from behind the counter. Kate's visits were still something of a rare occurrence and as there was much news to be had of the local inhabitants, by the time she had completed her shopping list, and bade Emily farewell, almost an hour had passed.

Fortunately her departure coincided with the arrival of Edwin Jameson accompanied by Doctor Parkins and helpfully Edwin assisted in placing her laden basket upon the back seat of his car.

"Ah, Katherine my dear, how good it is to see you out of the surroundings of the farm, why you blossom like a flower in the sunlight," Parkins stated cheerfully.

Kate felt a rush of colour to her cheeks. "You flatter me dear Doctor but I must confess to the enjoyment of it." She laughed.

"It is not flattery my dear I assure you. Do you not agree with me Mr Jameson?" Parkins turned at once to Edwin for confirmation.

"I agree wholeheartedly," Edwin replied, gazing at her features favourably.

Kate's eyes held his momentarily. "Now you have both conspired to heighten my cheeks with colour." She smiled, raising the fullness of her dress as she stepped carefully into the waiting car.

Edwin shook the doctor's hand. "Thank you for your assistance Sir."

"A pleasure my dear boy. Happy to have met with you." He turned to Kate, "I shall call as usual tomorrow my dear, meanwhile safe journey to you both." With a broad smile upon his face he waved them out of sight.

"The doctor is a good friend?" Edwin enquired casually, as they wend their way once more through the open countryside.

"Yes, for many months now." Kate nodded, "He worries about me in a most fatherly fashion."

"It is comforting to have such friendship; possessions are nothing to such a gift," he stated sombrely and for a moment, oblivious of the companion at his side, Edwin stared intently at the road ahead.

There was a hint of sadness in his voice which prompted Kate to turn towards him. "Why you must have many friends," she remarked encouragingly.

"None with such genuine concern as the good doctor's," he answered, shaking his head.

"Have you no wife Mr Jameson?" Kate asked with innocent curiosity.

Edwin found her frankness refreshing. "I fear I have had neither time nor inclination to devote to any woman," he said, glimpsing the query in her brown eyes. "No," he stated firmly, "work has always been sufficient for my needs."

"Perhaps the future will hold someone who will turn your head from business matters," she offered brightly.

"Perhaps," he reiterated, warming to her light hearted comment, "until then, would you be my friend and begin by calling me Edwin?" The suggestion was a spontaneous one, reflecting his unusual mood and suddenly fearing the request too presumptuous, he cleared his throat noisily to cover his unease.

His sudden display of vulnerability intrigued Kate, for whilst she understood only too well the subject of loneliness, it was difficult to accept that this man, of obvious means, did not lead life to the full. She hesitated, eyeing him quizzically. "If you wish it Edwin, yes, I would like to be your friend."

Delighted by her answer, Edwin decided to take the matter a step further. "The good doctor called you Katherine. Might I also presume the same familiarity?"

Kate sensed no undue forwardness on his part and in an effort to put him at his ease released a warm smile. "You," she replied in a positive manner, "may call me Kate."

"Kate," Edwin mused, "Kate, yes I like that and now formalities are at an end might I draw the car to a halt and stay awhile to savour a breath of air before returning you home."

Kate nodded her head in agreement and a moment later the car came to a halt at the roadside. Moving quickly to her side Edwin assisted her from the passenger seat.

"The sunlight is very strong Edwin take care lest it be too much for you," she suggested in a maternal fashion.

"I see that already our friendship has begun in earnest," he replied, laughing with pleasure as he loosened his tie and placed his jacket over the car seat.

"You seem much younger than you first appeared," Kate remarked candidly, observing his movements with interest as she seated herself on the wooden platform of a nearby stile.

"Ah, but when we first met, I had the officialdom of chambers about me. Now," Edwin inhaled deeply, "now I have pleasure in the escape of it."

"Then you should journey into the countryside more often Edwin," she smiled, "it so obviously suits you."

"Indeed, I would enjoy that," he replied, leaning against the fence beside her.

"My late father often spoke of city men who acquired cottages in the country for weekend purposes. You should do likewise," she proposed lightly.

Edwin gazed up at the cloudless blue sky and pondered thoughtfully upon her remark. "What a splendid idea," he said, turning his face towards her, "I shall stay a few days longer and begin my search."

"It was but a suggestion Edwin," Kate replied, somewhat startled by his fervour.

"Why I could purchase a cottage, install a daily woman to see that it was kept in good order and bring my painting materials with me," he rambled on optimistically.

"You did not speak previously of your own abilities on canvas," Kate remarked impressed by the knowledge.

Edwin's grey eyes glinted mischievously, "Ah now Kate," he replied, placing a finger upon his lips in a secretive fashion, " that my dear is a confidence only you and I will share, apart from Mrs Kemp, my daily help in London, who cleans the untidiness I also create."

Amused by his furtive manner Kate tossed her head back and released a ripple of laughter. The sound of it lingered and danced upon the warm air and Edwin, captivated by her femininity, took pleasure in the moment.

"Why the woman mocks me," he jested, feigning a hurt expression.

Kate's laughter subsided. "Mock you? Oh no, Edwin, I am merely bemused by the swiftness of your decision."

Edwin reflected upon the statement. "I must confess to generally being a man of careful deliberation, but today...today," he emphasised, inhaling deeply and stretching his arms luxuriously into the air, "I feel the need for change, after all, I am no longer a young man, in truth I am ageing by the minute."

Strands of unruly blond hair had wafted across his forehead, softening the soberness of his features and a smile that had tarried at the corner of his mouth erupted with playful effervescence. In truth, he was a most engaging person Kate mused and she sensed in him a stability and strength that bore the promise of a valued friend. Nonetheless, how she wished that it were Charles standing before her now. Then, casting selfish thoughts aside, she smiled at Edwin encouragingly.

"It is never too late for things to be altered," she stated, recalling how but a short time ago an outing such as this would have been impossible. Suddenly reality loomed. "What time have you Edwin?" she asked, waiting anxiously as he extracted a heavy gold watch from his waistcoat pocket.

"Quarter past four," he replied, aghast at how swiftly the hours had passed.

"Then I must return home for I have already been away far too long." With the tips of her fingers Kate raised the hem of her dress, before moving gingerly from the stile. With an admiring glance Edwin extended his hand to steady her descent and together they stepped toward the waiting vehicle.

"The afternoon has been most pleasurable Kate," Edwin remarked as he assisted her into the passenger seat, "perhaps in the near future, you might accompany me again?" His alert grey eyes questioned hers in hopeful anticipation and a smile creased his face as he rested his elbow leisurely upon the open door.

"I would be delighted Edwin and should you become a weekend neighbour I pray that you will visit often, but first let us see what property comes your way," she concluded matter-of-factly.

Enhanced by the heat of the afternoon, a colourful glow illuminated Kate's delicate features and wisps of glossy black hair that had loosened from the rest, hung attractively about her ears. Edwin lingered at her side aware of intense emotions awakening within. Indeed, such was his hesitation that Kate's brown eyes gazed at him quizzically.

"Edwin?" she queried softly.

At once his thoughts dispersed and with renewed enthusiasm, he moved to the front of the car, cranked the engine and climbed into the driving seat.

CHAPTER FIVE

For Edwin, the following weeks became a time of anticipated joy. No longer wishing to remain in the confines
of his apartment, he looked forward with youthful
exuberance to Friday mornings whereupon, he would
hurriedly attend to the paperwork upon his desk. Then
with an overnight bag at the ready he would journey
with reasonable speed to reach his destination, the
'Coach and Horses' in Hengleford, which in his opinion
provided accommodation second to none.

Upon Edwin's arrival Landlord Simms a giant cavalier of a man with a bushy beard and fun loving eyes,
would with regularity inform him as to the whereabouts
of vacant properties in the area. Indeed, such was the
friendliness of Simms and his plump, laughter-riddled
wife Mary, the welcome received upon each return
could be likened to that of the prodigal son, with many
of the locals gathering to relate happenings in the village
during his absence. That Edwin took pleasure in such
socialising would have been news less than credible to
his brother's ears and indeed many of his business asso-
ciates, but this was a life severed from the mustiness of
chambers and over the weeks his respect and admiration
grew for the straight talking manner of Northamptonshire
folk. Charles, in amazement, had approached him more
than once upon the subject of his weekend escapades
but Edwin remained silent as to the true purpose.

In reality he knew not which was the most exhilarating, the search for suitable property, or the prospect of visiting Kate at Pembleton farm where he had become a frequent visitor.

With each encounter they spoke of business matters and book keeping but when more pleasurable topics invaded their conversation neither seemed to tire of the other's company, in truth, for Edwin, the hours would pass with frightening swiftness. With chameleon like qualities he adapted to the climate of thought and hardship of those around him and should Albert, Kate's foreman, require assistance when others were not available, then eager to learn of husbandry Edwin would set to and labour with gusto. Kate made no mention of his brother, indeed she had not enquired after him since their first meeting and it was a silence by which Edwin was most encouraged.

It was late August, when Edwin found it necessary to call at Pembleton farm with documents urgently requiring Kate's signature. As his car was undergoing repairs, the garage proprietor loaned him his own treasured vehicle, an Argyll 25, which had a sturdy body and was perhaps more suited to the long trip in changeable weather.

Indeed, there was a chill in the air and the brightness of the sun lacked the heat of previous days. As it was Thursday his arrival had been totally unexpected. But nonetheless, by late afternoon he stood sipping tea and gazing out of the cottage window whilst Kate attended to the needs of her husband.

Suddenly, at the sound of a shrill cry from the bedroom above he placed his teacup on the table, bounded up the narrow wooden staircase and moving through an open doorway on the left, found Kate crouched over the waxen figure of Jack Pembleton. It was Edwin's first glimpse of his client since some two years before and the dramatic change from strength to weakness in the man prompted in him a momentary shudder. Crisp, white bed linen accentuated the sallowness of the old man's skin and there was an aura about the room that needed no explanation.

Treading quietly over the linoleum floor Edwin placed his hand at Kate's elbow and moving her gently aside picked up Pembleton's thin, scrawny wrist from under the bed covers. He could feel no pulse and on opening the old man's night shirt, knelt over the bed to place his ear at the cage of protruding bones. "I fear the end for him has come my dear," he murmured, raising his head. In a reverent manner he adjusted the coverlet over the still figure and on rising to his feet drew the curtains at the casement window to a close.

Kate stared impassively at the outline of her husband's body beneath its shroud. How much in life she had feared this man and yet at this moment his passing bought little relief, only a sense of guilt. To suit his purpose Jack had offered her wedlock and in order to escape poverty and despair she had proved a willing victim. Who then bore the shame of it, he for asking, or she for such a ready acceptance.

"Come Kate," Edwin coaxed, resting his hand gently upon her shoulders, "there is no more to be done." Then, taking her hand in his he led her down the staircase towards the fireside chair in the living room. Kate's face was ashen and once seated, she shivered involuntarily. "Have you brandy in the cupboard?" he asked quietly. She shook her head. At once Edwin hurried to the car and a moment later returned with a flask in his hand. Compassion flooded his grey eyes as he knelt before her. "Here my dear, drink some of this." Kate raised the flask to her lips and sipping from it choked upon the sharpness of the liquid. "I shall fetch Albert so that he might stay with you whilst I go for Doctor Parkins," he said, turning to leave.

"No Edwin," she pleaded quietly, edging forward upon her seat, "I would rather you stay. Let Albert go for the Doctor. He can take the pony and trap."

Doctor Parkins was about to settle down for his afternoon tea when Albert knocked urgently at his door. At once he reached for his bag and a short time later they arrived at the farm. News of Pembleton's passing was of little surprise to the astute, kindly practitioner and after a brief examination of Jack, he descended the stairs to confirm to Kate, what in effect she already knew. "Do you wish Dora to stay the night with you Katherine?" he offered quietly, resting his hand lightly upon her arm.

Dulled by the occasion, Kate's eyes stared vacantly into his. "Thank you, but there is no need," she whispered.

"Very well my dear. I will not stay myself as there is much to be done. Leave the funeral arrangements to me. I shall provide a death certificate and see to all that is necessary." With a chubby hand he gave her shoulder a comforting squeeze, then turned anxiously to Edwin. "How fortunate that you are here. Will you stay awhile?" he asked removing the stethoscope from around his neck and snapping his bag to a close.

"Of course," Edwin nodded solemnly, "and if there is any way in which I can be of assistance, you have only to speak of it," he offered. A moment later, deep in thought, Edwin accompanied the doctor over the threshold and once outside in the cobbled yard, he closed the door behind him. "Doctor Parkins, I have no wish to pry into Pembleton's private life, but rumours of past injustices to Kate...." Edwin broke off, reluctant to speak out of turn.

Before he could continue further Gerald Parkins nodded his head knowingly. "I understand my boy. Indeed I bear no ill will towards the departed, but alas," he sighed, "though I shudder to say it, I am certain the farm will be a happier place for his passing. Katherine has suffered."

Albert's approach with the pony and trap cut short the doctor's confidentiality. "Suffice to say death numbs the spirit in the living however much it is expected. Look after her Edwin, for both Dora and I have developed a great affection for her."

After escorting the doctor safely on his way, Edwin returned to the cottage to find Kate still seated by the unlit fire. With head bowed and hands resting calmly in the cradle of her lap, she appeared detached from the happenings around her and at that moment, Edwin had doubts as to her awareness of his presence. Suddenly she raised her head and the look of vulnerability in her deep brown eyes, stirred within him such passion that his body trembled in the wake of it. Then she shivered, due to shock he suspected and moving swiftly to her side, he placed the warmth of his hands, over the coolness of her own.

"I'll stay awhile Kate," he said quietly, "but should you wish to retire early then speak of it. In the meantime I shall prepare a hot drink for you."

The tension in Kate's body eased as she surrendered to his benevolence. "Dear Edwin, how grateful I am that you are here," she murmured, lifting the palm of his hand to her face and resting her cheek against it. In the fading light of the room, Edwin knelt before her, the longing inside him almost unbearable, but alas, this was not the moment in which to speak his thoughts aloud. To detract from his yearning he gently loosened his hand from her grasp and put a match to the fire.

Upon return to chambers Edwin's first undertaking was to ask Miss Bartholomew to bring in Pembleton's safety deposit box from the storeroom and any other files pertinent to their client. Half an hour passed by when there was a light tapping at his door and his ever efficient secretary entered, her arms overloaded with several files and the appropriate box. "Here, let me help you Miss Bartholomew." Edwin arose hurriedly from his chair and removing some of the files from under her chin, turned to place them upon his desk.

"Will there be anything else Mr Jameson?" she asked as she placed the deed box beside the papers.

"I think that will be all for now." Edwin looked up and smiled appreciatively, "until coffee time."

No sooner had she left the room than Edwin began to sift through all the information concerning Jack Pembleton, member of the parish of Hengleford. In due course all the paper work he examined confirmed that there were no other living relatives to be notified of his demise, so it would appear that Kate was the sole beneficiary of the farm and any other assets accumulated over the years. He wondered briefly how a man living in such squalid conditions could have proven such an astute character with regard to investments, though concerning his financial outgoings he understood from Albert that little had been spent on the farm in recent years, save for the re-stocking of cattle.

A large buff coloured envelope revealed the deeds which had originally belonged to one Thaddeus Pembleton, who from the various birth and death certificates attached, established the man to be Jack Pembleton's father. Further information confirmed that the dwelling and a specific amount of acreage had been gifted unconditionally to Thaddeus Pembleton in gratitude of his extraordinary bravery, but as to the details of the former, none could be found. There was little reference to his wife Elizabeth, Jack's mother, save the fact that she had died of consumption in her early thirties. Having died intestate, Jack Pembleton could have caused something of a dilemma beyond his grave. Fortunately, throughout the man's illness a number of papers had been signed and witnessed with regard to Kate and the solicitors to act on his behalf, so Edwin could not foresee any complications arising.

The funeral of Jack Pembleton took place just over a week later and but for Kate, the farm hands, Doctor Parkins and Edwin who made the impromptu journey, there were no others in attendance. To save unnecessary distress, Doctor Parkins' wife had prepared tea in her own parlour and upon the party's return from the cemetery, she hovered attentively at Kate's side.

Dora Parkins was a small, rounded motherly figure, with curly snow-white hair and a fresh colour to her cheeks. As fate would have it she had no children of her own, and from the moment her husband had confided in her news of Kate's circumstances, she had seen fit to take the child under her wing. Later that afternoon, when the farm hands had departed the premises, she approached Katherine. "Katherine my dear," Dora began cautiously, smoothing the freshly ironed apron about her waist, "the time has been a trying one for you of late. Would you not reconsider the possibility of a short holiday? September can be such an invigorating time of the year and a few days at my cousin's house by the coast would help you face the long winter months ahead."

Kate turned to Edwin who sat quietly at her side. "Yes," he confirmed, noting her pallor, "a taste of sea air would restore the colour in your cheeks and we can delay matters of business until your return."

With so much to be done, Kate had little desire to leave the area at present, but too weary to offer any resistance she succumbed to the wisdom of her companions. "If you all recommend it, I shall be ready to accompany you Dora by, shall we say the end of September?" she replied, knowing full well that arrangements could be left in their capable hands.

It was almost six o'clock in the evening when Gerald Parkins, engrossed in conversation with Edwin, was suddenly interrupted by a request to visit a sick patient. "Will you see Katherine home Edwin? One never knows how long these visits of mine will take me."

"Have no fear," Edwin replied amiably, "I shall attend to it and perhaps as you will be a grass widower of sorts in a few weeks, we might take advantage of each other's company. After all, the enthusiastic ear in my search for property will be travelling to new horizons."

"Good idea my boy, we'll have a bite of supper together at the Inn. No doubt I shall be in need of a few hearty meals with my good wife away," he concluded, shaking Edwin's hand warmly.

An hour later, after thanking Dora for her assistance throughout the day, Edwin escorted Kate to his car and drove her back to Pembleton farm. As he opened the door of her cottage, Kate swayed unsteadily on her feet. "Kate my dear, what is wrong?" he queried as he helped her inside and seated her gently into the fireside chair. Still overwhelmed by an attack of dizziness, she gave no answer.

The premises appeared somewhat chilly for the heat of the day had long departed and whilst it was still light outside, corners of the room remained in darkness. "Let me return for Doctor Parkins," he suggested, swiftly lighting an oil lamp before turning to leave.

"No Edwin," Kate pleaded, holding up her hand, "there is no need, I am sure this feeling will pass." He stooped before the mantelpiece to put a match to the fire made ready and when it finally took hold turned towards her. A little colour had returned to her cheeks and she smiled back at him reassuringly. "I am well now Edwin, it was but a temporary lapse after the effort of the day." She looked so alone, so vulnerable he thought and concern etched his features as he moved to her side. "You are overdoing things Kate," he chided softly, "you need someone to take care of you."

The gravity of the moment was quickly dispersed by her smile of amusement. "And who pray would accept such a responsibility," she enquired lightly.

He sensed her change of mood and answered accordingly. "I myself would not be averse to the challenge," he quipped, testing her reaction.

"Dear Edwin." She sighed, uplifted by his support.

Inspired by her not unfavourable response Edwin's voice took on a more serious tone. "I know the time is not appropriate for me to speak of such matters, but in truth Kate, from the moment we first met I have thought of you not only as a friend, but one with whom I would wish to share my life." Perturbed by Edwin's unexpected outburst of emotion Kate moved her lips to speak, but before she could do so he gestured her silence. "Pray allow me to continue my dear, for I shall not raise the subject again." Suddenly aware of his own fortitude, he nervously cleared his throat. "Whilst you are away, would you consider my words as a proposal of marriage, for as one who loves you deeply, I would be honoured to spend my life devoted to making yours a happy one."

Tears welled in Kate's eyes as she returned his stare. What could she say that would not hurt the feelings of so dear a companion? He knelt before her and as she cupped his head between her hands, her fingers followed the outline of his strong features. "Oh my dear Edwin," she hesitated, wishing to find the right and proper words, "you are a good friend and I bless the day we first met. I care for you a great deal and am profoundly moved, indeed honoured by your words, but it would be wrong of me to give you hope that we could be anything other than devoted friends. I wish with all my heart I had not cause to hurt you so," she concluded sadly.

Edwin took her hands into his own. "I understand," he sighed, rising to his feet, "but should you have need of me for anything in the future, do not allow my disclosure to deter you from the asking." Then, in an attempt to conceal his disappointment, his voice took on a lighter tone. "Take care upon your journey my dear," he concluded, bending forward to place a kiss upon her cheek,

"I shall eagerly await a letter that will inform me of your travels and who knows, upon your return perhaps a cottage of my own will be seeking your approval."

"Upon arrival I will write you at once," she promised, "if only to say how much I miss your presence."

Edwin winced, sensing pity in her words and as he moved to the door his grey eyes glistened with emotion. With quiet deliberation he lifted the latch of the door, then, hesitating turned to face her. "One day Kate I shall attempt to capture you on canvas," he said softly. And forcing a smile he bade her goodnight.

Upon Edwin's departure an aura of sadness filled the room and long after he had gone, Kate still seated by the fire, reflected upon the kindness this gentle person had shown her these many months past. He was a good, sensitive, caring man and in thought and conversation they had much in common. Indeed she might even have considered sharing in his future had his brother Charles not entered her life. The truth of it was, she still yearned for sight and sound of her erring love. Why, she knew not, for in her heart of hearts, she sensed that he had little intention of ever returning. Indeed, if he did so, the seeds of doubt had already been sown and such misgivings would not allow her to resume the affair. No. The burden of love was an undertaking too painful to endure she mused sadly and she had no wish to submit herself to such intimacy again. Nonetheless, an image of Edwin's dear face remained with her and before retiring she made a mental note to write to him as promised upon her arrival at Dora's cousin's house.

The days passed by swiftly and soon preparations for the holiday were complete. On Saturday morning at seven o'clock Gerald Parkins and his wife arrived at Pembleton farm to collect Kate and her belongings. After last minute instructions to Albert, Kate finally made ready to leave and soon the doctor's car was wending its way towards the railway station, situated a short distance down the road.

Once enclosed in the warmth of the railway carriage, Dora's enthusiasm proved infectious and Kate, in fairness to her companion, made an effort to cast her own cares aside. Upon return there would be much to decide upon, but, for the present she would give herself fully to the period of rest that lay ahead. The train chugged noisily through the undulating countryside belching thick grey smoke into the chill air of the September morning and in no time at all, the motion of the carriage prompted Kate to close her eyes. Presently, exhausted by events of the past weeks, she fell into a deep sleep. From her seat opposite, Dora eyed her protégé in a maternal fashion. A nap would do the poor child good she reflected and extracting a book from the laden basket at her side, remained silent for the rest of the trip.

At journey's end Dora's cousin Victoria and her husband Reginald Hamilton greeted them both in a grand fashion and after a speedy introduction, they were quickly ushered into a waiting car. The Hamilton's were a handsome couple and though retired and in their sixties, they exuded an effervescence which belied their years and indeed, such was their openness that by the time the party reached its destination, Kate felt truly at ease in their company. It was almost two o'clock when they reached the steps of the Regency town house situated opposite the promenade and whilst Reginald Hamilton removed their luggage from the car, Victoria, in order that they might freshen up in preparation for some light refreshment, promptly led her guests up the wide stairway with its highly polished mahogany bannister and along a spacious landing to their respective rooms.

Kate's brown eyes widened with surprise when escorted over the threshold, for her accommodation was immense, or so it seemed after the tiny rooms to which she was accustomed. Rich, red velvet drapes hung luxuriously from a tall, broad window overlooking the sea front and to the left in a corner, stood an elegant writing desk with tapered legs and inset of red leather. Someone had thoughtfully placed pen and ink beside a generous measure of paper for convenience. A few feet away, a gleaming brass bedstead with a thick feather mattress raised high above the oak floorboards, bore a cover of delicate lace and in a fireplace of white marble, coals burned brightly, extending warmth into the atmosphere.

"It's a delightful room." Kate enthused and Victoria, pleased with her efforts of the past few days, preened with satisfaction.

"Through here is your bathroom Katherine," Victoria continued, proceeding to open a slightly smaller door off to her right, "and now I can boast that there is constant hot water." Kate stepped forward, her eyes agog with disbelief. Such luxury was beyond all expectation.

At that moment Dora tapped her door and entered. "Victoria my dear," she remarked excitedly, "your premises are positively palatial."

Victoria laughed aloud. "Had you visited two years ago it would not have appeared so, but at that time, with Reginald's retirement imminent we decided to make life as comfortable as possible and the result I think has been worth all the inconvenience." Her companions agreed wholeheartedly and without further ado Victoria left them to freshen up.

That evening, after dinner, Dora began to enquire about the general health of other distant relatives, whereupon Kate, having no wish to intrude upon family matters, made her excuses and retired early.

Undressing by the luxurious warmth of the fire, Kate sat in her night attire to write as promised to Edwin of her safe arrival. Never have I seen such beautiful objects she began. I am sure that you would also appreciate their true value. The house is large, the rooms spacious and many, but each bears the warmth and personality of our hosts, a most entertaining, generous couple. Indeed, though I confess I was at first reluctant to visit, already I find myself stimulated by the jolliness of their company. An hour later she sealed the envelope. After brushing her teeth in the sumptuous bathroom with its gleaming brass faucets, she returned to set the coverlet of the bed aside and to ease her body between the crisp linen sheets.

At half past eight the following morning, as previously arranged, Kate entered the dining room for breakfast to find her hosts discussing with great enthusiasm an invitation just received by special messenger. The invitation, extending to their guests, was to a Ball at Harlestone Manor, some five miles into the countryside and the news prompted a whoop of delight from the excited Victoria.

"Yes it will undoubtedly be a grand affair." Reginald confirmed, fingering his tight moustache thoughtfully.

His insistence that they should all attend caused some alarm. A plea from Kate that she had nothing suitable for such an occasion was at once dismissed by Victoria who quickly set about arranging a shopping expedition for the following day and as Dora also found herself in the same predicament, it was decided they should all go together.

The rest of Sunday was spent in a leisurely manner which bore no particular pattern or routine and to Kate proved a welcome escape from the strict timetable adhered to at Pembleton farm. After lunch Dora and Kate responded eagerly to Victoria's suggestion for a breath of air, whilst Reginald, seated in his comfortable armchair, declined good naturedly seizing on the opportunity for a short nap.

When the party set off along the lengthy promenade there was little heat to be gained from the late September sunshine, however, they were suitably dressed in warm clothing and soon the invigorating exercise brought a healthy glow to their cheeks. Almost an hour had passed by when the sun, weak as it was, disappeared from the sky completely and ominous clouds gathered on the horizon. The cold grey waters of the North Sea suddenly lashed with force against the jetty and as rain began to filter through the air, the ladies, in full agreement, quickened their step and hastened back to Reginald and the cosy warmth of the fireside.

Soon Monday morning was upon them and dreary though the weather was, it did little to dampen the spirits of Victoria. "The clouds will soon disperse," she announced confidently as she spread a generous helping of marmalade upon her toast. Kate smiled knowingly across the table at Dora and their eyes met in confirmation. If Victoria willed it, it would be so, as she had a certain flair for organizing and in all probability her powers extended to the weather.

Nonetheless, Kate observed her hostess with admiration. For this tall, elegant woman with lively blue, eyes and silver grey hair swept high upon her head, possessed the self-assurance of a general leading his troops to victory. Indeed, in her presence, one had the unswerving conviction that, should a catastrophe occur, it would be dealt with and swept aside before realised as such.

"More tea?" Reginald queried, peering at Kate over his newspaper.

Her thoughts dispersed and smiling graciously, she placed her cup and saucer into his outstretched hand.

"No doubt you are looking forward to your shopping spree eh young lady?" he chuckled.

In truth, until now, Kate had given it little thought.

"Of course she is Reginald," Victoria stated assertively, "and Dora too I suspect. After all there is little opportunity for such a pleasurable jaunt in Hengleford is there?"

"You have visited the area then Victoria?" Kate questioned.

"Oh yes my dear, many years ago, though I daresay it is very much as it was. Am I right Dora?"

Dora nodded her head in agreement. "Yes, but then we enjoy the peace and tranquillity of it, do we not Katherine?" she stated, looking to Kate for support.

Victoria grimaced. "You are but a child Katherine. How can you bear such solitude. I'd die, just die, simply from boredom."

Reginald laughed aloud. "My dear, that you could be bored anywhere is a statement I will not accept." His eyes caught Katherine's. "Do not allow my wife's frivolous manner to fool you Katherine, for many years ago, whilst I was serving in the Guards, we travelled abroad extensively and on occasion found ourselves in some very remote areas of India."

Victoria's cheeks heightened with colour. "Hush Reginald, I am sure Katherine has no wish to hear of such things."

Reminded of Rudyard Kipling's novel Kim, Kate was at once intrigued by an image of Victoria in such circumstances and urged Reginald on.

"My wife was a tower of strength," he continued proudly, "not only to myself but numerous inhabitants of poor standing. Indeed, until Victoria's arrival, villages close by were ill equipped to combat infection and many lacked sufficient medical supplies."

"Reginald," Victoria interrupted firmly, "that is quite enough. Why you'll have Katherine thinking I was some kind of Florence Nightingale."

"To many you were my dear," he continued fondly.

The Hamilton's devotion to each other was total and as Kate listened to their cheerful banter, she thought it a pity that their marriage, like Dora's, had not been blessed with children, for what an abundance of love and security they would have lavished on their offspring.

A further two hours passed by before Reginald finally prised the ladies from the breakfast table, by which time, as Victoria had so confidently predicted, the rain had stopped and beams of sunlight flooded through the dining room window. Having prepared the motor vehicle for its journey into town, Reginald quickly deposited them at the steps of Victoria's dressmaker and with a promise to return at three o'clock in the afternoon, sped quickly out of sight.

The dressmaker's display window was small, showing accessories such as handbags, shoes, gloves and jewellery. Once one crossed over a threshold separated by green velvet drapes fringed with gold tassels however, they found a long, narrow room that extended to the back of the shop. It housed a surprising array of dresses, silks and satins to titillate the eyes of the beholder. Silky cream paper patterned with tiny, delicate flowers lined the walls. Ornate Regency cheval mirrors were placed in positions suitable for clients to view what they were wearing from every angle.

Kate caught her breath at sight of the modelled gowns. Then, a moment later, with a mixture of delight and apprehension, she moved across the room and proceeded to run her fingers over the delicate materials. At this point Victoria excused herself from their company and left to speak with the proprietor, Madame Gaskell, an elegant woman of French origin. A short time later, Victoria returned displaying a confident smile. "Now my dears," she murmured discreetly, "as you were both unprepared for such an outlay on your visit I have taken the liberty of having the cost of your garments placed on my account. I insist," she concluded, waiving aside their protests, "the matter is closed."

It was a thoughtful gesture, one that was greeted with some relief by both Dora and Kate. And with their minds unperturbed by the possibility of any financial embarrassment, they gave themselves wholeheartedly to the task in hand. At Madame Gaskell's signal, her assistant provided tea and a generous slice of gateau in a comfortable room adjoining the premises. It was there that the group began in earnest to discuss suitable materials and eventually have their measurements taken.

With regard to the ball, time was of the essence and the prospect of altering some gowns already prepared for a fashion event in October was talked about more fully. Then there was a choice of colour and style.

True to his word, Reginald Hamilton collected them at precisely three o'clock and whisked them home in time to rest in the parlour before changing for dinner. "Well Katherine," Victoria began as they seated themselves by the fire, "I eagerly await your views on Madame Gaskell's premises."

"Never have I seen so many materials under one roof," Kate enthused, "in truth, it was like stepping into Aladdin's cave."

"I knew you would appreciate the experience," Victoria's eyes sparkled, "and Madame's ability with needle and thread is beyond reproach my dear. I have no doubt that after only one fitting your garment will have the makings of perfection." Of the latter Kate had no misgivings. However, as the day of the Ball drew closer, the splendour of the occasion was beginning to cause her some alarm.

"Is something troubling you my dear?" Victoria asked, noting the look of anxiety upon Kate's face.

"The ball... I have never," Kate hesitated and lowered her eyes, "I cannot dance." she blurted, her features flushed with embarrassment at the declaration.

"Ah," Victoria gave a sigh of relief, "for a moment I thought the problem a serious one."

"But surely," Kate began in earnest.

"Elizabeth shall teach you," Victoria interrupted confidently, rising from her chair, "perhaps three or four of the most popular dances will suffice for the occasion."

"Elizabeth?" Kate queried.

Victoria paused over the threshold of the parlour and turned towards her. "Mrs. Bolton's daughter," she explained. "They are close neighbours. At present she is the Operatic Society's choreographer and after Christmas departs for a post in London. If I arrange it would you be willing to see her?"

Joy illuminated Kate's face. "If you think I would benefit from instruction with so little time."

"Without doubt," Victoria confirmed, "you have an ear for music and I have seen your feet tapping to the recordings on our phonograph." Then with a satisfactory nod of the head she departed.

Dora smiled knowingly at Kate, "I have a feeling that the next few days will be somewhat hectic for you Katherine."

"Perhaps the lady in question will be too busy to..." Kate broke off at the sound of Dora's laughter.

"Tut tut Katherine," the doctor's wife replied, wiping tears of mirth from her eyes with a crisp white handkerchief, "Victoria has already decided upon the outcome, the young tutor will be putty in her hands."

A short time later, Victoria re-appeared in the doorway of the parlour, a triumphant glint in her eyes.

"Well?" Dora and Kate chorused.

"Ten o'clock tomorrow morning at the Exhibition Hall off Regent Road," Victoria whooped with delight. "Elizabeth will be awaiting your arrival Katherine. I understand the Operatic Society do all their rehearsing there, so it is well equipped."

Dora smiled. Her cousin had a kind heart and she had already done so much to make their stay a happy one, "Well done Victoria," she enthused gratefully.

"I only hope that I'll be worthy of the task after all the trouble you have taken," Kate concluded.

"Of course you will my dear," Victoria replied, "and now I must find Reginald to tell him of your appointment. He will be only too happy to see that you arrive on time."

As Dora had predicted, the days preceding the ball were hectic ones for Kate. She enjoyed the company of Elizabeth, who proved an excellent teacher and the hours spent under her tuition, though exhausting, were most rewarding. Indeed, whilst Kate had not previously spoken to Dora and their host of her apprehension regarding the protocol on such occasions, such was the strength of her new found friendship that she felt able to confess it to Elizabeth. She at once offered information on the routine happenings at such an event, which all proved sufficient to set Kate's mind at rest. Elizabeth's thoughtfulness also extended to borrowing a long silk evening gown for Kate from the Operatic Society's bulging wardrobe, so she might become accustomed to the length and sensation of it as she practised her movements around the dance floor.

So the day of the Ball arrived and after a prolonged visit from Victoria's hairdresser, who attended to all the ladies, the household settled down to partake of afternoon tea in the warmth of the parlour. It was now October and a grey afternoon to boot and as they sat in comfort by the glow of the fire, Victoria's revelations of previous social events induced something of a party atmosphere. Indeed, such was the happy group's euphoria that when Reginald broke into their conversation, suggesting it was time to change, the ladies made their way upstairs with a certain reluctance.

Nonetheless, as Kate moved over the threshold into the quiet of her bedroom, she welcomed the brief period of silence. The luxury of her own bathroom, with its endless supply of creams and toiletries added to the pleasure of her preparation. Indeed, the release from chores upon the farm, plus the daily application of various creams upon her hands proved beneficial too, for the redness of them had begun to fade and they felt much smoother to the touch.

Removing her day clothes, she wrapped a large, soft blue bathrobe around her body and seating herself before the mirror at the dressing table, eyed her jet black hair with more than a little trepidation. The severe style she was used to had been replaced by a softer, gentler one. Delicate ringlets framed her face and with great skill the hairdresser had swept back her hair and created a mass of curls high upon the back of her head in order to accentuate the sleek line of her slender neck. The result was indeed most pleasing Kate thought and as she placed a touch of rouge upon her cheeks, a suggestion Victoria had made earlier, the importance of the occasion suddenly overwhelmed her and a feeling of excitement smouldered within. At the sound of a light tapping upon her door, Kate quickly placed a shawl about her shoulders and moved across the room.

It was Matilde, Victoria's maid, a willing young girl slightly younger than herself. "Mistress thought you might need some assistance with your gown," she offered cheerfully.

"Oh how thoughtful," Kate said with obvious relief, "I would appreciate some help."

By now, partly clothed in the new undergarments that Victoria had recommended, she turned and moved towards the dressing table. Matilde, stepping on tiptoe, reached into the large wardrobe and carefully removed the dress of beech brown silk interwoven with gold thread, from its hanger. At once her deft fingers quickly unfastened the buttons at the back of the dress that continued all the way down to the waistline.

"There," Matilde sighed after concluding the task, "now I'll hold it out for you Miss, whilst you step into it. That'll be the easiest."

Carefully Kate did as she suggested and as they lifted the bodice of it upwards over her breasts, she slipped her arms into the long sleeves of luxurious silk. Soon the high collar rested at her throat and once in position, the maid was behind her, fastening the discreet buttons that followed the outline of her spine. When the task was done, Kate cast a critical eye over her image in the cheval mirror and with a radiant smile upon her face found the result gratifying.

"Oh Miss," Matilde's pale blue eyes shone with admiration. "you look a treat if I may say so."

Kate's face flushed with colour. "Thank you Matilde and also for your assistance, I can't think how I would have managed without you."

"It's been a pleasure Miss," she replied, as she handed Kate her gloves and delicate purse.

Kate smiled her appreciation and taking a deep breath left the bedroom to seek approval from her companions.

"You look like a goddess my child." remarked a buoyant Victoria as Kate entered the room. "I'm so pleased we dissuaded you from wearing black. Oh, I know it's the chosen colour under such circumstances, but who will be aware of your circumstances in tonight's company."

Kate, looking a little apprehensive turned to Dora who nodded approvingly.

"You look a picture my dear. If Gerald and Edwin could see you now they would delight in the spectacle."

"Hear hear," Reginald confirmed, "by jove, what a lucky fellow I am, escorting three such splendid ladies."

The ball was indeed a glamorous affair, so much so that even as Kate stepped into Lord Harlestone's opulent entrance hall, her confidence began to wane. Now all too vividly she recalled the squalor she encountered on her arrival at Pembleton farm and the burden of life she had to bear with Jack Pembleton. This evening's occasion was a far cry from such happenings, but in many ways both accounts seemed unreal, imaginary. With a look of bewilderment clearly showing upon her face, she observed the finery of the people around her and as the sound of the orchestra's fine tuning reached her ears, there was little thought in her mind save the knowledge that she was truly outclassed in such wealthy company.

Victoria was at her side and having sensed her discomfort squeezed her arm lightly. "Hold your head up high and be yourself my dear. You outshine them all," she whispered confidently. The remark was a genuine one. For Victoria was not given to idle flattery. However she was curious to see how her young protégé reacted to high society and therefore followed her movements closely.

Heartened by Victoria's words Kate took a deep breath and a moment later advanced with decorum into the crowded ballroom. Her appearance did not pass unnoticed, indeed by the time Reginald had located their table and distributed glasses of punch, acquaintances were intrigued sufficient to approach their corner.

Observing the proceedings with relish was Edward Harlestone, at nineteen, the youngest member of the hosting family. He was a fine boy, though somewhat encumbered by extreme height and a lean matchwood body. His manner too lacked the confidence enjoyed by many of his contemporaries. Nonetheless, from the moment of their introduction he had watched Kate with all the fascination of an enamoured youth. Now, as he edged his way through the throng to claim the first waltz, a measure of welcome instigated by his father earlier, he fought to overcome his nervousness. A sombre dress suit with white shirt and black bow tie accentuated his gangling youthfulness, but in truth, as he approached Kate's side and reminded her of the request, such admiration oozed from his cherubic features as to detract from his gawky physique. Kate's deep brown eyes melted at sight of him and aware that his sensitivity and awkwardness matched her own, responded to his plea with a warm hearted smile.

Victoria's face beamed with pleasure as she observed young Harlestone escorting Katherine onto the dance floor. "What a beautiful young woman Katherine is," she murmured to Dora, seated at her side. "Intelligent, receptive, socially acceptable in every respect, yet you say her short life has been a troubled one?" She raised her eyebrows in disbelief.

Dora hesitated. Whilst not wishing to disclose more of Katherine's personal affairs than was necessary her cousin had gone to great lengths to make their visit a successful one and it was plain to see that she too had become fond of the girl.

"Come Dora," Victoria urged, "it goes without saying that whatever you choose to tell me will be treated in the strictest of confidence."

The latter was true. Her discretion was never in doubt. Whereupon, Dora proceeded to enlighten her with relevant details regarding Jack Pembleton. When she had done her companion's face clouded with concern. "The poor child," Victoria began sympathetically, but before she could say more Katherine approached with her escort and hurriedly she changed the subject to lighter matters.

Flushed from the effort of dancing Kate seated herself beside the ladies, whereupon young Harlestone, still basking in the glow of her undivided attention, arranged another dance on her card then excused himself temporarily from their party and retreated discreetly into the background. Victoria's bright blue eyes twinkled with amusement as she watched his exit. "So, the ardent admirer departs to reflect upon his moment of glory no doubt." she murmured to Kate.

Kate smiled happily, "At sight of so many lovely young ladies about the room, I fear my image will soon be replaced by that of another," she remarked philosophically.

At which point Reginald, who had been circulating, returned to their table with news of recent happenings in the city. After a short reference concerning acquaintances who had lost relatives on the ill-fated liner 'Titanic' earlier in the year, conversation turned to events of which Kate had little knowledge. But the short respite from dialogue gave her the opportunity to absorb in silence the magnificent room with its huge marble pillars and bright chandeliers. It was truly an evening to remember and whilst she had no desire to attend such functions with regularity, she was obliged to the Hamilton's for this brief glimpse of opulence and splendour. As Kate watched bejewelled ladies in glittering finery move graciously from one group to another whilst their male counterparts hovered with glasses of punch and offered witty repartee, it appeared like a scene from a play, unreal, without substance.

The approach of a smiling escort suddenly dispersed her wanderings and in the hours that followed she participated in the revelry with enthusiasm and vigour. Kate would have been less than human if she had not been flattered by her new found popularity, but, when a brief interval was announced shortly after eleven o'clock, she welcomed the opportunity to relax with her companions and observe once more other groups at their leisure.

It was then that she saw Charles Jameson. He was standing but ten paces away, surrounded by a throng of young ladies vying eagerly for his attention. Kate caught her breath, startled by his unexpected appearance. Victoria heard her gasp and turning towards her nudged her elbow gently. "Is anything amiss my dear?" she queried. Kate stared ahead oblivious to her request. Whereupon Victoria, curious as to the cause of her companion's awesome gaze, followed its source and on seeing the gallant Jameson understood the reason for it. "Yes, he is a handsome fellow is he not Katherine, Reginald will arrange an introduction if you wish."

Before Victoria could finish her sentence Charles Jameson, having glimpsed their party, approached with an engaging smile upon his face. "Mr Hamilton, Mrs Hamilton." He nodded graciously as he extended his hand. "A pleasure to meet with you again. The Hunt ball was the last affair I believe."

Reginald nodded affably and after introducing Dora they turned in unison towards Kate. A flush of colour heightened her cheeks as Jameson's eyes sought hers.

"But we have met have we not Mrs Pembleton?" he confirmed lightly. "Though alas not under such pleasant circumstances." He gathered her hand into his own and squeezed it lightly before releasing it. After a brief explanation to the rest of the company he turned to Kate and queried with a smile. "If you are free to do so, may I have the pleasure of the next dance Mrs Pembleton?"

Kate had no wish for it but a blunt refusal on her part would have attracted the attention of others, and so, when the interval was over she allowed him to escort her on to the floor. A moment later, amidst the crowd, they turned to face one another.

Jameson viewed her in a leisurely fashion. "You look absolutely stunning Katherine," he concluded admiringly.

"Thank you Mr Jameson," she acknowledged coolly, hoping to discourage further conversation by her aloofness.

Amused by the formality of her reply the hint of a smile crossed his lips and Kate, aware of his charisma, began to tremble at his nearness. Suddenly the orchestra began to play and his outstretched hand reached for hers.

"I must see you alone," he murmured, drawing her into the circle of his arms, "if only to explain the agonies of my decision not to contact you again." A sombre frown creased his forehead and the deep blue of his eyes bore a doleful plea as he looked down upon her.

"There is no need for explanation," she replied lightly.

"But Katherine, you must allow me the opportunity to defend my actions," he argued gently.

"The matter is of no consequence," she stated, turning her head deliberately to acknowledge other dancers as they moved around the floor.

A hurt expression flooded Jameson's handsome features. "Then the pleasure we shared so briefly is already erased from your memory?" he quizzed.

Kate's cheeks heightened in colour and piqued by his lack of discretion her brown eyes glinted at him defiantly. "Erased no put aside yes," she remarked curtly.

Jameson looked at her approvingly. This was a new, confident Katherine and her indifference was a challenge he could not resist. "I have hurt you deeply I know," he continued, choosing his words with care, "but circumstances have changed somewhat since our last meeting, so please I beg of you Katherine, allow me to make amends."

The request bore a note of genuine remorse and despite Kate's efforts to withstand his beguiling manner she felt weakened by it. She raised her eyebrows inquisitively, "And how could you do that pray?"

That he had caught her interest was an encouraging sign, but alas, before he could continue further, the music came to an end. With a teasing smile he whispered hurriedly, "We shall see."

On escorting Kate back to her table Jameson expressed his regret to all at having to return to his own party. Then much to Kate's surprise, with a respectful nod of the head in her direction, he bade them all a polite farewell and promptly disappeared into the crowd. A moment later Kate's eyes searched the room for sight of him, but he had vanished completely. He was a will-o-the-wisp she mused bitterly and his appearance then sudden evaporation was proving a disarming habit. Moreover, when she sought to erase him from her mind and recapture her carefree mood, all pleasure was lost by the unexpected confrontation.

It was in the early hours that the Hamilton party finally bade farewell to their hosts and stepped into Reginald's car that had been driven to the front of the house for their convenience. All were weary and but for an occasional comment echoing through the darkness of the vehicle, much of the journey homeward was spent in silent assessment of the evening's entertainment. Once they reached home they all agreed to air their views on the evening's highlights at breakfast later that morning. Somewhat exhausted, each ascended the stairs to their various rooms. Before retiring Dora stepped briefly into Kate's bedroom to assist in removing her gown, then anxious for her own bed bade her goodnight.

Exhausted as Kate was, when she eventually eased her body between the sheets of the comfortable bed she was restless and could not sleep. Indeed, as she stared wide eyed into the darkness of the room, events of the evening overcame her and once more she was plagued by an image of Charles Jameson. Many times she had envisaged such a meeting and after so long a spell thought to remain unmoved by the experience, but his manifestation at the ball had caught her totally unprepared. In truth, she was physically shaken by the feelings his presence evoked.

From the moment of their first encounter at Pembleton farm she had, like a zealous juvenile, been bedazzled by his charm. Whilst the latter did not condone her reckless behaviour, she experienced a modicum of comfort at recollection of the females on the dance floor eagerly seeking his attention. There was no denying he was a handsome figure with great personal magnetism and whilst she was now painfully aware of the fickleness of his character, she was nonetheless consumed by a yearning to be in his company once more.

The moon, full and round, shone like a beacon through the large bedroom window and in the quiet of her room Kate's mood oscillated between longing and frustration. Had her aloofness that evening caused him genuine concern? Would the status of widowhood encourage him to seek a further rendezvous? Ah, what fantasies the mind doth weave when ruled by matters of the heart.

It was almost three o'clock in the afternoon when Herbert Clitheroe, a long standing business associate of Reginald's called upon the Hamilton's expressing a desire that they and their charming guests should spend the weekend at his house in the country. Kate and Dora had planned to return to Hengleford this very Saturday, yet both were anxious not to spoil a pleasant weekend for their hosts, who after all had seen fit to ensure that they had had a wonderful holiday. With the latter in mind they discussed the subject openly and after much deliberation, with Victoria's encouragement, telephoned Dora's husband suggesting their departure be delayed until the following Tuesday. After an exasperating time with one telephone operator after another, Dora finally spoke to her husband. Gerald Parkins assured her at once all would be well and that he would contact Albert personally at Pembleton farm to give him the news. Then, after a hearty endorsement with regard to their plans, he wished them all an enjoyable weekend.

Later, over tea in the parlour, Victoria's enjoyment at keeping her guests for a little longer was obvious. The hum of excited chatter filled the room as the ladies contemplated the weekend ahead. Indeed, all agreed upon return from the Clitheroes that the extra day would allow sufficient time for the packing of suitcases and any last minute shopping necessary.

With the burden of farm duties eased from her mind, Kate too began to savour the prospects of a lengthier visit. And when Victoria took her by the hand and insisted on helping her choose her wardrobe for the occasion, she warmed once more to the consideration and thoughtfulness of her generous hosts. "Anything lacking can then be acquired tomorrow," Victoria assured her affectionately as she ushered Kate up the stairs to her bedroom. Needless to say, a short visit to Madame Gaskells in search of items of country attire was required.

With uncanny swiftness Friday dawned. As the party motored to the Clitheroe's residence, the journey proved a pleasant excursion into the autumnal countryside. The cool, crisp morning air was more in keeping with December, although the sun shone from a cloudless sky adding a richness of colour to the amber browns of the season. The drive was a leisurely one, spent in pleasant conversation and almost two hours had passed before Reginald Hamilton veered off the main road to manoeuvre the vehicle through the narrow leafy approach to the Clitheroe's sprawling grounds.

As they emerged from the sheltering archway of trees, the house came into view and both Kate and Dora caught their breath in astonishment. This was not the insignificant hideaway either had envisaged. Indeed, the ivy covered Manor House, with its gables and sloping buttresses was a most impressive building.

It was evident from the bustle and activity in the large, circular driveway that other guests had already arrived and no sooner had the Hamilton's car come to an abrupt and somewhat noisy standstill, than a uniformed chauffeur approached to remove their luggage and drive their vehicle to a spacious parking area. A moment later their hosts, a jolly couple from the north of England, appeared on the steps of the ornate porchway to welcome them.

Reginald had confided earlier that Herbert Clitheroe was a self-made millionaire and a ruthless competitor in matters of business, which was difficult to believe when confronted by the man, for his rustic open features and ready smile revealed nothing but an easy going nature. Bess, his wife, was of the same robust stature, with rosy red cheeks and strong, muscular limbs that showed little signs of femininity. Her voice however, was surprisingly soft and articulate and in greeting bore little trace of humble beginnings. As they stood side by side, the couple's mannerisms were noticeably alike, an index finger raised to trace the line of the left eyebrow, the enthusiastic gesticulating of hands and arms. Perhaps thirty years of wedlock had encouraged the similarities Kate mused thoughtfully as she ascended the steps. It was then she glimpsed the figure of Charles Jameson, standing discreetly in the background. At sight of him her heart leapt. Had he instigated the invitation she wondered. Her pulse raced as they exchanged glances.

"You all know Charles, my right hand in legal matters," Herbert Clitheroe commented as he ushered them through the spacious hallway.

"Ah, we meet again, so soon," Reginald stated. The group nodded their heads and smiled in affirmation.

"Well now," Clitheroe beamed, rubbing his hands together vigorously, "Bess will show you to your rooms and after you have freshened up you must come and meet our other guests."

Other guests numbered five. Colonel and Mrs Jessup, their daughter Emily (a plain woman in her thirties) and Mr and Mrs Hargreave from Halifax. After introductions, an assorted tray of drinks were distributed throughout and the Clitheroes invited the party to help themselves to the appetizing buffet luncheon close at hand. It was an informal affair and soon the large oak panelled room with its roaring fire and variety of deep, winged chairs, together with an enormous sofa, buzzed to the sound of light-hearted chatter.

The guests were not as illustrious as Kate had first suspected and on occasion she took pleasure in absorbing the friendly opulence of her surroundings. Without careful planning the mere size of the room could have discharged a somewhat sombre atmosphere, instead, however, her hosts had complemented the highly polished dark floorboards with a scattering of colourful Persian rugs and displayed an interesting selection of photographs and objet d'art, to create a homely appearance.

In a quiet corner Reginald and Charles had become engrossed in Herbert's plans for the following day's activities and eventually, when sunlight began to fade from the French window overlooking the terrace, Mr and Mrs Hargreave suggested a hand or two of bridge with the Colonel and his wife. Dora, who had been admiring the colourful houseplants in the room, spoke of her passion for flowers and shrubs, whereupon Bess Clitheroe, delighted to find a gardening enthusiast like herself, invited the remaining ladies into the orangery. Emily Jessup declined and for reasons best known to herself, kept close vigil at her parent's side.

There were twelve in all for dinner that evening and as the Clitheroe's led the party into the dining room and settled their guests at the table, Kate found herself seated opposite Charles Jameson. Throughout the afternoon his manner had been polite though somewhat distant toward her and in truth Kate was bemused by the fluctuating hot and cold of his attentions. Now however, with little else to distract him, his charm came to the fore and as he looked across the table, his deep blue eyes penetrated hers.

"And how are you enjoying your visit to the coast Mrs Pembleton?" he queried genially.

"Very much, Mr Jameson," Kate replied, returning his stare with a confidence she was far from feeling.

A smile tweaked the corners of his mouth. "Charles please." he insisted, and with his eyes still upon her he reached for his wine glass and began to sip his claret.

The colour rose up in her cheeks and as she looked at him it was as if her own naivety was reflected in his stare. "Very well... Charles." she stressed in a condescending manner before lowering her gaze.

"The sea air is not too invigorating I trust," he continued playfully.

"On the contrary, I find it most stimulating," she retorted.

"And the delightful coastal villages hereabouts. Have you visited many?" he quizzed.

Kate's slender fingers toyed momentarily with the stem of her wine glass. "Unfortunately no, but then time has passed so quickly."

Charles turned to Reginald seated to his left. "So your guests have not yet sampled the neighbouring county's coastline Mr. Hamilton?" he chided.

"Alas no," Reginald confessed apologetically.

"Then perhaps I could drive them to Southwold on Monday?" Charles prompted, "It would be a pity to return to Hengleford before viewing the lesser known promenades along the coast."

"A splendid idea Charles, eh Victoria?" Reginald queried turning to his wife for confirmation.

Victoria, who was talking to Bess Clitheroe at the time, had caught little of their discussion. Nonetheless when the idea was put to her she agreed wholeheartedly.

"That's settled then," Charles beamed, returning his gaze to Kate, "I'm sure you will find the experience a rewarding one and Mrs Parkins too of course," he added politely, casting a glance in Dora's direction.

A charismatic smile endorsed his eagerness to please and suddenly Kate's efforts to maintain a frosty aloofness seemed but a futile exercise. Indeed, in an atmosphere of such conviviality a truce was inevitable and in answer, the tautness of her features relaxed into a smile.

"Then I shall look forward to Monday Mr...Charles." she replied softly.

Sensing appeasement Jameson resumed his gallant air, "Then may I presume to call you Katherine?"

Kate cringed momentarily on recollection of a similar request at Pembleton farm and once again her cheeks flooded with colour. His cavalier manner was perplexing to say the least and sensing a hint of mockery in his voice she glanced furtively at her companions, but all were engrossed in conversation.

"Well Mrs. Pembleton?" Charles prompted gently.

His look conveyed a desire for reconciliation and it would have been churlish to deny the overture. She nodded her head lightly in acquiescence and for the first time since their encounter at the ball, began to relax in his company.

The weekend proved a huge success especially for Kate, as the limited circle of friends she once enjoyed had widened into new horizons. The Clitheroe's plainly approved of Kate too, for her genuine interest in all around her made a refreshing change from the decorative, but empty headed young ladies usually adorning their table at Charles Jameson's suggestion. On this occasion their young colleague had introduced a charming newcomer, pleasing to everyone and indeed such was their regard for Kate that upon her departure they extended a carte blanche invitation for her and Dora to visit whenever they wished.

It was after Sunday lunch that the parties finally bade their farewells and dispersed. Charles who was staying the extra night with their hosts, escorted Kate and Dora to the Hamilton's car and with a promise to call for them at ten o'clock the following morning, returned to the steps of the portico to wave them a cheery goodbye. Kate watched attentively through the car window as he accompanied their hosts back into the house. Could this be her last glimpse of him? Would he suddenly be called elsewhere, or perhaps, bored by his commitment for the morrow, simply telephone his regrets. In truth, with regard to Mr Charles Jameson one never knew.

En route homeward Dora felt unwell. She was on occasion prone to attacks of migraine and though she had suffered rarely of late, was aware of the symptoms before leaving the Clitheroes. From that moment on her eyes grew heavy and as the pain in her head worsened, her only wish was to take to her bed and remain in a darkened room. Victoria at once urged Reginald to make haste and for the rest of the journey, out of consideration for their companion's malaise, there was little conversation between the parties. As if in sympathy, the once bright blue skies became overcast and low lying thunder clouds bore the promise of rain. However, the roads were clear, with little traffic and shortly after six o'clock they reached the familiar surroundings of the Hamilton's abode.

No sooner had the vehicle come to a standstill than Victoria rushed into the house to ask Matilde to prepare a hot water bottle for Dora's bed and whilst Kate assisted her friend from the car, Reginald promptly removed their weekend cases from the rack attached to the back of the car. Minutes later Dora was safely over the threshold, whereupon Victoria, in her usual competent fashion, took charge and ushered her up the stairs.

"Dora's in good hands my dear," Reginald stated confidently as they moved into the parlour to warm themselves by the open fire.

Kate was all too aware that Victoria would be at her best tending the sick and with a knowing smile began to reflect aloud upon the pleasurable weekend.

"I take it that you thoroughly enjoyed the experience Katherine?" Reginald commented, grateful that it hadn't been too much of an ordeal for her.

"Very much," Kate enthused as she seated herself opposite him by the fire, "I can't thank you and Victoria enough for all you have done to make this holiday such a pleasurable one."

"Well you surely did us proud my dear and by no means must this be your only visit. Whenever time allows you must return. Without doubt your company will be missed at any future engagements we attend."

Colour flooded Kate's cheeks at the compliment.

At that moment Victoria entered the room and sank gratefully into an easy chair. Reginald turned to his wife, " I was just saying to Katherine that invitations will be abound requesting more of her company, do you not think so my dear?"

"I do," Victoria emphasized, "and have you made it clear that her presence is welcome here at any time?" she prompted.

With an agreeable smile Reginald glanced at Katherine." We have discussed the matter haven't we my dear?"

"We have," Katherine reiterated, "and I was saying to Reginald earlier, that I'm indebted to you both for making my stay here such a memorable one."

"No need to say more," Victoria interrupted, "your visit has revitalized us both has it not Reginald?"

"I heartily agree." he confirmed, rising from his chair and moving towards the decanter resting on a small round table in the corner of the room. "Now would you like a sherry my dear and you Katherine? I can highly recommend it and it may be one of the last opportunities to raise our glasses together for a while."

After a friendly toast, Victoria assured them that all was well with Dora, but, she added, "It's clear that she will be unable to accompany you tomorrow Katherine."

Reginald sighed sympathetically and moving from the heat of the fire, stepped forward to collect his unopened newspaper from the sideboard.

Disappointment flooded Kate's being. The fates were cruel indeed, for if Charles kept his word, it now appeared they would not meet again. Suddenly her concern for Dora's wellbeing surpassed any selfish desire. "Then we must cancel the trip," she began, bravely concealing her regret.

"Cancel," Victoria repeated aghast, "heavens no my dear, you must go as planned, the excursion will be good for you, after all I shall be here to attend Dora."

A perplexed look clouded Kate's deep brown eyes. "But Victoria," she protested.

"Now now," Victoria chided, "no buts my dear. I insist you make the most of what promises to be an interesting day."

"But would it be ..." Kate hesitated.

"Would it be what my child. Out with it." Victoria urged gently.

"Appropriate as such, to go unaccompanied." Kate blurted.

Victoria's laughter rippled through the air. "Oh my dear Katherine this is not the dark ages and you are not surrounded by the villagers of Hengleford. Charles Jameson is a personable young man. A rascal for the ladies I grant you, but no harm should come to you throughout the daylight hours. " Her lips broadened in a smile of amusement. "Come now," she murmured reassuringly, "put all doubts aside whilst we discuss what you are to wear."

Shortly after supper Kate spoke of her wish to retire to bed early. It had been an exhausting weekend she confided and she would have a long day ahead of her tomorrow.

Victoria agreed. There was wisdom in the suggestion of an early night. "Indeed," she yawned, glancing at her husband seated comfortably in his favourite deep winged chair, "I'm inclined to follow your example and leave the Master of the house at peace with his newspaper."

Reginald glanced across at his wife affectionately. "You go up my dear I'll be with you shortly."

Whereupon Victoria raised herself from her chair and accompanied Kate up the stairs. "I shall look in on Dora before retiring so goodnight to you Katherine. Sleep well," she murmured in parting.

Kate opened the door of her bedroom and as she crossed the threshold, the warmth of the brightly burning fire came to meet her. For a moment she stood before the mantelpiece staring at the coals, not wishing to move. Then, out of necessity, with slow deliberation she began to undress. Presently her gaze shifted to the writing bureau and she caught sight of an unfinished letter to Edwin that she had begun a few days before. Guilt irked her conscience and smitten by self-reproach her features took on a troubled air. Dear Edwin, with so much activity over the past few days she had neglected to write further of her movements. Would the good Doctor oblige by giving him an account of recent happenings she mused.

Her mind flitted from one subject to another in a restless fashion. Poor Dora, perhaps a good night's sleep would rid her of her dreadful complaint. Perhaps tomorrow. Ah tomorrow… A faraway look invaded her eyes as she lingered fancifully upon the moment of Charles Jameson's arrival. What would be his reaction to the news that she was to be his only companion for the whole day. Would he approve? Disapprove? The uncertainty of it all prompted a mixture of excitement and apprehension to surge through her veins. What was it about this man that intrigued her so. Indeed, his appearance now proved nothing but a shameful reminder of her foolish indiscretion, yet in truth, she glowed inwardly in his presence and was, in a curious manner, stimulated by his company. Suddenly the clock on the pedestal table at her side chimed ten and as the melodious tones broke into her reverie, she pulled back the bed covers and eased herself onto the luxurious warmth of the mattress.

Monday morning arrived and bright sunlight streamed through the bedroom window as Kate prepared for the day ahead. Originally she had brought a limited choice of garments to wear on holiday, but before their stay at the Clitheroes, Victoria had surprised her with two brand new outfits for daytime wear that Madame Gaskell had especially chosen for Katherine. Both were gifts from Madame personally by way of repaying Victoria's kindness in promoting her business to friends in the area. After much deliberation Kate chose the cream silk blouse that fastened high up to the neck, with delicate lace discreetly covering the button holes at the front. Then stepping into the warmer of the lengthy check woollen skirts she eyed herself in the mirror to make sure that all was satisfactory. Before going down to breakfast, she slipped quietly into Dora's bedroom, but her companion was fast asleep and having no wish to disturb her, Kate continued quietly down the wide staircase.

Her hosts, having risen early, were already eating and as Kate entered the room they greeted her in unison with encouraging news of the day's weather. "You have been most fortunate with the climate during your stay Katherine for early October can be particularly fickle in these parts."

"I think I have been blessed in many ways," Kate responded. "It's difficult to imagine that by this time tomorrow Dora and I will be preparing to leave."

"All the more reason to take pleasure in today's activities," Victoria replied.

Kate glanced instinctively at the clock on the mantelpiece.

"It is only nine o'clock my dear," Victoria confirmed noting her young friend's anxiety, "there is ample time for a hearty breakfast before you leave."

Kate's stomach fluttered nervously at the reminder of Charles Jameson's impending arrival and as she eyed the array of dishes on the sideboard she concluded aloud that toast would be more than sufficient.

Promptly at ten o'clock Charles Jameson arrived.

When the doorbell rang, Kate was upstairs collecting the smartest, though alas not the warmest coat she possessed from her wardrobe. It was left to Reginald Hamilton to explain why their cousin would be unable to take advantage of the day's outing.

In her usual hospitable manner Victoria invited Charles into the comfort of the parlour and all were engrossed in conversation when Kate finally appeared. Jameson's eyes lit up momentarily acknowledging her presence and a sympathetic frown crossed his brow as he spoke of his regret for Dora's malaise.

Victoria, worried that Kate would be tempted to forego the trip, promptly reassured her that she would take good care of their patient. Then, anxious that the young ones make the most of the fine weather she ushered them quickly to the front door. The sun was still shining but there was a distinct chill in the air and as Kate stepped outside the house, she pulled the collar of her coat close about her neck for protection from the gusty wind.

Aware of her discomfort Charles hurried down the steps to the waiting vehicle and after assisting Kate into the passenger seat, quickly moved around the front of the car and seated himself beside her. A moment later the engine roared to life with a spluttering, noisy invigoration and with a cheery wave to Victoria the couple set off.

Soon the promenade was far behind them and as they wended their way through the open countryside, Charles gave an interesting account of the buildings and churches thereabouts. His own interpretation of history and the like was peppered with amusing anecdotes and before long Kate's apprehension of the day was muted by the pleasure of his lively company. Indeed, had Charles Jameson's attraction relied solely upon his handsome features one would perhaps have looked upon him less favourably, but in truth, his sense of humour and sheer gusto for life ranked him an excellent companion, adding a richness to his character that made his charm all consuming. At times he was a boy, bubbling with energy and inquisitiveness and once again Kate, the innocent bystander, found herself under the spell of his charisma.

En route there were few vehicles to deter them from enjoying the scenery and about a mile and a half away from their destination, Charles suggested they might call upon his friend John Trimble whose cottage was but a short detour. "The property was bequeathed to him by his late uncle and needed much in the way of renovation to make it habitable," Charles continued enthusiastically, " however, colleagues inform me that..." He stopped mid-sentence, aware of her silence.

GILL CROSS

"Of course should you wish to go directly to Southwold then we will do so," he confirmed sharply, concentrating on the road ahead as he awaited her answer.

Had he mistaken her innocent day dreaming for inattentiveness Kate mused. Having no wish to offend she turned towards him in her seat and commented eagerly, "Oh no, I was merely thinking that the builders might not appreciate our presence."

"Builders?" Jameson queried, glancing quizzically in her direction. "Oh, I see. Did I not make it clear Katherine, John has been doing the work himself throughout his holidays and at the weekends?

"Ah," Kate nodded her head in understanding, "then of course we must see the cottage," she concluded with a smile.

Her companion reiterated with a gesture of satisfaction and a quarter of a mile further along the main road they veered to the left down a narrow winding lane. The end was almost in sight when a car approached from the opposite direction.

"I do believe it's the master builder himself," Charles exclaimed, promptly drawing the car to a halt and alighting from it.

The driver of the other vehicle, a tall fellow with a military stance and short cropped fair hair did likewise. After pausing for a moment to finger the upturned edges of his generous moustache, he gave a smile of recognition and bound fitfully towards Charles.

"Charles old chap how good to see you," Trimble retorted, his deep voice resonating through the air as he shook his friend by the hand. "I was just about to drive the good lady and myself back to the city. There is a function we must attend there tomorrow."

"Ah, pity," Charles broke in, "I had thought to show off the fruits of your labours to an acquaintance of mine whilst we were in the area."

"Then carry on old chap. The keys are over the back door. We leave them there for Mrs Thomson. She lives in Southwold and calls on Tuesday mornings to give the place a general tidy up before we return at the weekends."

"But..." Charles remained hesitant.

"Please, I insist," Trimble remarked encouragingly, "providing you place the keys back where you found them." Then, with an anxious frown he lifted the pocket watch attached to a gold chain strung about his waistcoat. "Heavens" he grimaced, "is that the time? Well, mustn't delay or it'll be dark before we arrive back home eh?" Whereupon, he raised his hand in a mock salute toward Kate and with a nod of farewell to Charles hurried back to his car. Seconds later he reversed, allowing sufficient room for them to pass by.

Charles stood in the middle of the lane observing his friend's manoeuvre when suddenly a forceful wind billowed his jacket and shivering in the cool air he rubbed his hands together and quickly returned to his seat beside Kate. "It is somewhat cooler now than earlier this morning Katherine. Will you be warm enough?" he asked, casting his eyes with some misgivings over her light, worsted coat.

The wind howled relentlessly around the vehicle and momentarily Kate too had her doubts. But bolstered by his concern for her welfare, she responded with an agreeable nod. "Have we far to go?" she asked.

"No," he replied amiably, releasing the handbrake, "we should get our first glimpse of the property quite soon."

The car rolled forward and with a wave of his hand to the Trimble's in passing, they reached the bottom of the lane and as they slowly turned the corner Charles gave a sigh of satisfaction. "Well?" he queried, searching Kate's face for signs of approval as he applied the handbrake.

The trim, thatched cottage stood several yards back from the road and but for a narrow white gated entrance, the property and garden in front of it was surrounded by a four foot high stone wall. Relief plaster decorated the front and end gables of the premises, whilst gleaming, white paint covered the window ledges above and below to frame a picturesque mesh work of leaded glass panes. The front oaken door was sheltered by a quaint, rustic porch way while on either side of the narrow pathway leading to the gate, rich brown soil, freshly dug, had been left to lie fallow in preparation for spring planting.

Kate's eyes shone with delight. "Oh Charles, it is lovely," she commented enthusiastically.

"I wonder if the interior will match up to this?" he continued thoughtfully. "We shall see. You wait here whilst I go for the keys."

Kate watched as he moved out of sight. With a sigh of contentment she leaned back in her seat to observe the cottage unhindered. Moments later Charles returned, brushing brick dust from the turn-ups of his beige, cavalry twill trousers.

"Perhaps this was not such a good idea after all." He grinned impishly, opening the car door and extending a hand towards her.

"Oh, why is that?" Kate queried.

"Trimble's cleaning lady must be of amazon

proportions," he stated, waving a bundle of keys playfully in front of her face. " To retrieve these I have just climbed a rubbish mountain that falls little short of Mount Everest."

Kate laughed openly, "Then I congratulate you upon your accomplishment," she remarked good humouredly, alighting from the car.

"What, no special reward?" Charles trifled, feigning dismay.

Their eyes met and lingered in an intimate fashion. Then, a sudden gust of wind propelled Kate backwards against the car, freeing her from his riveting gaze.

"Come," Charles laughed, beckoning her up the path, "before you catch your death."

Although he had dismissed the moment in a casual manner Kate's relief was only temporary. As they moved over the threshold of the cottage his body brushed against hers and she was conscious of the fact that no other dwellings were close at hand, indeed, they were truly isolated.

"The place is surprisingly cosy." Charles commented, bounding across the freshly distempered room towards the inglenook fireplace. Removing the poker from its stand he prodded the dying embers of a fire. "Are you sure you are all right Katherine?" he queried, turning towards her and studying her face with empathy.

If you only knew, Kate agonized silently. "Mm," she murmured aloud, rubbing her arms vigorously through the loose, wide sleeves of her coat in order to generate warmth.

He held out his hand, coaxing her towards the remains of the fire. "There is still some heat to be gained from it," he remarked encouragingly, "would you like to stay here whilst I look around?"

Kate shook her head in a contrary fashion and concealed her disquiet with a smile. "Having come this far it would be a pity to miss the extent of your friend's efforts," she replied, skirting her way around tea chests placed indiscriminately about the floor.

Charles grinned at the tenacity of his companion. "As you wish," he beckoned. "Follow me."

Together they lowered their heads under the newly restored oak beams and as they eased their bodies between the disarray of furniture, Charles, with the expertise of a house agent, proceeded to give a light-hearted narrative as to the advantages and dis-advantages of such a property. But for items of little consequence the renovation appeared complete. Kate began to remove her shoes for fear of leaving grime on the newly laid rugs at the bottom of the stairs.

Her companion watched with interest, gathering pleasure from her feminine movements. "What a considerate young woman you are," he commented, offering his arm to steady her in the task.

Kate warmed inwardly to the gesture and every word he uttered. Then, with a spurt of confidence she expressed a Tut of mock disapproval at sight of his dusty brogues.

"I take it you wish me to do the same?" he reflected, shamming dismay.

Her eyebrows arched in a reprimanding manner, yet there was a smiling affection in her deep brown eyes. "It would be prudent," she concurred patiently.

The tantalizing simplicity of her actions aroused Charles instantly. What a provocative creature she was he mused. His eyes followed the contours of her grace-ful neck and as they came to rest upon her chaste, maidenly features, a querulous expression crossed his handsome brow. "Tell me," he quizzed, placing a hand upon her shoulder for support as he removed his shoes, "would you take such steps if this was our cottage."

Kate sensed an overture of intimacy and feeling ill equipped to answer, turned from him in her embarrassment.

"Well?" he urged, placing the palm of his hand upon her cheek and guiding her face towards his.

Kate made an effort at flippancy, but his closeness was an overpowering magnet of pleasure and pain that deemed her impotent. In truth she was mesmerized by his presence and when his arms began to encircle her body, her heart pounded.

"Oh Katherine," Charles whispered softly, "do you know how often my thoughts have lingered upon such a moment?"

"Please, I beseech you," she pleaded, writhing from his embrace, "do not trifle with my affections again. I could not bear it."

A gleam of victory erupted in his deep, blue eyes. "Oh, my dearest one, I have no intention of trifling as you put it," he stated earnestly. "You are free now are you not, to pursue our friendship?"

Kate stared at him incredulously. "Yes, but..."

Charles laughed aloud at her awe struck features, "Yes, dear heart, I mean that if you wish me to court you in an honourable way then I shall do so. But..." His eyes simmered with passion as he replaced his hands upon her shoulders and drew her closer.

"But..?" Kate echoed.

He smiled at her accusingly. "I must confess your nearness stirs my senses and I..." His unfinished sentence drifted upon the air as he leaned forward to place a kiss upon her ear lobe. Then suddenly he released her and as his arms fell loosely to his sides, he hung his head in a self-effacing manner. "Forgive me," he murmured apologetically, " I..."

The gesture of humility was more than Kate could bear and instinctively she reached out in a comforting fashion and closed her arms about the nape of his neck.

"Oh Katherine," Charles groaned, "I will not deny that other women have entered my life, but none, I swear, have inflamed me so."

Kate stared at him in wonderment, her mind devoid of questions and reproach. She assumed, indeed, had no reason to doubt, that he loved her now and the knowing of it was sufficient to justify all that had gone before. Suddenly the tautness of her features relaxed in a joyous smile, and when he gathered her into his arms and his lips found hers, she was lost in a sea of ecstasy.

Presently he released her and bending his head to avoid the low slung stairwell led Kate up the steep, narrow staircase. "These premises are positively rife with danger," he quipped. "How Trimble manages to escape permanent injury amazes me."

"Doubtless he is more familiar with such obstacles than you or I," Kate answered happily.

"Mmmm," Charles conceded and on reaching the landing hesitated to observe the two latched doors on either side and one door facing them at the end of the corridor. "Now what have we here?" The door on the left opened on to a small bedroom, freshly decorated but as yet unfurnished. The door on the right was a bathroom. "Somewhat basic I fear," Charles stated, eyeing the facilities with a degree of distaste.

Kate looked inside and it appeared to her something of a luxurious habitat. Indeed, if Pembleton cottage possessed such a room she would consider herself most fortunate. But then Charles, she suspected, would be unaware of such crudities as tin baths and water pumps. The latter was a point that caused her to ponder on the differences of their backgrounds. However, her thoughts quickly dispersed when Charles walked to the far end of the landing and opened the door facing them.

It was of generous proportions and so obviously intended to be the Trimble's bedroom. The curtains were drawn and when he moved over to the window and pulled them aside, a stream of daylight revealed a stylish room, with rose covered wallpaper and gleaming white paintwork. Plain sheepskin rugs were strewn indiscriminately over the dark, wooden floorboards and on either side of the huge bed were small, circular tables complete with oil lamps and the usual paraphernalia.

Charles turned, his eyes scanning her features as he leaned casually against the window frame. "Well, what do you think of the cottage Katherine?

"I think your friend John Trimble must have worked very hard to achieve such splendid results," she replied from the open doorway.

"Come see the view from the window," he urged as he gazed with interest upon the surrounding fields.

Kate declined politely but firmly. "I have no wish to intrude upon the privacy of another's bedroom."

"You are right of course," he conceded. Then pulling the curtains to a close moved towards her as she awaited him on the landing. "My truly, beguiling Katherine," he remarked fondly, placing his arm about her shoulders and gently pulling her towards him.

Kate trembled at his touch. "Perhaps we should leave?" she began.

His deep blue eyes searched hers. "There is ample time. Southwold is but a short distance away. Could we not linger awhile so I might have you to myself a little longer?" he murmured persuasively.

Kate knew instinctively that the wisest thing to do was to insist upon leaving, but the warmth of him encompassed her and she had no wish to stir from the pleasure of his caress. A moment later Charles lowered his head and his lips sought hers with a fiery intensity. Kate, consumed by the flame of unrequited passion responded unashamedly. In his presence she was a juvenile and in her adulation for her handsome companion, she found herself once again, totally under his spell.

It was almost two o'clock in the afternoon when they left the cottage and finally made their way to Southwold. The wind had dropped and the air, though fresh, was less biting than earlier that morning. However, with only a short period left in which to explore the quaintness of the area before daylight faded, there was little time to lose. Neither had eaten since breakfast, but to save any further delay, they decided to take a late lunch at a teashop when the light finally faded. Having parked the car in a quiet cul-de-sac, Charles assisted her from the vehicle and with his hand at her elbow, guided her protectively along the seafront.

In his usual, informative manner he pointed out the lighthouse topped with a gold weather vane that stood sentinel over the town's rooftops and the battery of cannon on the green overlooking the sea front, sent by Charles I to protect the gracious village against privateers.

They moved through the cobbled back streets of red brick and flint cottages, where Kate was puzzled by the presence of numerous birds perched high on the leaded roof of a fine church nearby. She said as much.

"In search of food no doubt." he retorted, "before their lengthy flight to the coast of Holland."

Kate wondered briefly if it was not too late for such an expedition, but did not query the fact. Indeed, under such tuition she proved an attentive scholar and engrossed in her handsome companion's repertoire, failed to notice that daylight had all but disappeared. Nonetheless, when a magnificent dray horse, pulling a cart loaded with empty barrels passed them on its way back to the nearby brewery Charles broke off from his narrative to apologise for having delayed their late lunch. Eager to atone for such inconsideration, he guided her swiftly around the corner into a fashionable teashop.

At once Kate warmed to the open friendliness of the proprietor and in no time at all she was comfortably seated by a roaring fire and tucking in to a generous portion of home cooked ham and scrambled eggs.

From across the table her companion eyed her with fond amusement. "I should be horsewhipped for delaying sustenance to such a healthy appetite."

Kate raised her head and smiled across at him. "Do not reproach yourself, after all I have learned a great deal about an area that was quite foreign to me earlier this morning."

Charles placed his hand over hers and gazed steadily into her deep, brown eyes. "My dearest Katherine without doubt you are generous to a fault," he concluded, raising her hand to his lips.

She blushed in answer, but warmed to the intimacy of his voice.

For much of the journey homeward Kate was preoccupied. Marriage, the farm, and her future with Charles were thoughts uppermost in her mind. When Charles sought to draw her attention to a monument illuminated by the car's headlamps, she said nothing, but merely nodded her head in a reticent manner.

"Am I to assume by your silence that you are already regretting our indiscretion at the cottage?" Charles queried sharply, slightly irked by his inability to arouse her interest.

At once Kate's thoughts dispersed and she turned towards him in the darkness, eager to make amends. "Oh no, not at all. I was simply intent on plans for our future."

Her companion mellowed a little. "Ah, then just this once I shall excuse the diversion," he murmured benevolently, "however, it would be a pity to mar the day with practicalities. Could we not continue to enjoy the hours left to the full? There will be ample time for discussion when I visit you at the farm."

Kate moved her head to one side and stared at the shadow of him quizzically. "But I had thought to mention our news to the Hamilton's upon our return."

Charles shrugged his shoulders in an offhand manner as he stared at the road ahead. "As you wish my dearest, although I had proposed to keep the matter between ourselves for the present. It would be more prudent perhaps to hold back the news, being so soon after your husband's demise, and," he added lightly, "until I have purchased an engagement ring worthy of my devotion."

"An engagement ring!" Kate exclaimed excitedly. "In truth, I had forgotten such formalities." She sensed rather than saw his crestfallen features and wishing only to please him curbed her disappointment. "Then of course we must withhold the news," she said, " and we can speak of future plans when you visit at the weekend."

"The weekend after I'm afraid," he corrected. "On return to London there will be a plethora of business matters requiring my attention, and doubtless brother Edwin will already be gathering forces to have me hung, drawn and quartered for my being absent from chambers longer than I intended."

Kate's eyes widened with surprise for his words conjured up an unfamiliar image of the Edwin she knew. Dear Edwin she mused, how would he react to her news? "Your brother has always appeared a mild mannered personage to me," she remarked loyally.

"Of course, I was forgetting," Charles exclaimed, recalling Edwin's earlier visit to Pembleton farm, "you have met, have you not?"

"On many occasion," Kate confirmed readily.

Her companion's eyebrows arched in surprise as he pondered upon her statement. Then suddenly reality began to dawn upon him and a teasing expression pervaded his deep blue eyes. "Ah" he nodded presumptuously, "so you my dear are the reason for Edwin's fervent interest in rural affairs."

Kate felt the colour rise in her cheeks and at once the need to justify her actions became paramount. "As your brother was unfamiliar with the County I have assisted him from time to time in his search for property," she counteracted.

Charles beamed. At last he had discovered the cause of Edwin's unusual behaviour. "No doubt my sweet, he is as fascinated by you as I," he quipped and in her effort to reassure him otherwise, Kate failed to notice the gloating emphasis of his tone.

When they finally reached the Hamilton's residence it was almost ten o'clock in the evening. The sky was black, starless, and the moon skulked behind thunder-clouds that had threatened the area all day. Charles drew the car expertly to a halt and turning in his seat squeezed Kate's hand gently. "Take care, dear heart. I shall be with you as soon as I am able," he murmured reassuringly.

Still overawed by his attentiveness throughout the day, Kate studied his shadowy features in the darkness, knowing every inch of his handsome face. "I shall be waiting," she whispered, confirming her eagerness with a gentle pressure upon his hand.

Moved by her naivety Charles smiled at her fondly and later, with his hand at her elbow, he escorted her up the wide steep steps to the house. At the front door he leaned across her and pulled hard at the cast iron bell attached to the wall. Matilde wasted no time in answer-ing the call, whereupon with a polite farewell, Charles left Kate's side and hurried back to the car. Kate turned briefly to watch his departure, but aware that Matilde was waiting for her to enter the house, stepped quickly over the threshold.

"Good evening Matilde." Kate remarked happily.

"Evening Ma'am. Mrs Hamilton is in the" before she could continue Victoria breezed into the hall.

"Katherine my dear, we have missed you," she said, rushing forward to peck Kate's cheek. "Did you have a pleasant day? Somewhat blustery I fear. You must be weary, nonetheless I insist that you have a hot drink with us before retiring."

Victoria's openness accentuated Kate's feeling of regret at having to keep the news of her engagement a secret. However, the reason for doing so quickly relinquished any pangs of self-reproach and she smiled happily as she tarried under the glow of the hall light to remove her coat.

"My dear, you look radiant," her hostess exclaimed, "the day in young Jameson's company obviously suited you," she concluded, slotting her arm through Kate's in a sisterly fashion and urging her into the warmth of the parlour.

The light-hearted statement brought a flush of colour to Kate's cheeks. "How is Dora?" she asked, hoping to deflect the course of conversation.

Victoria's eyes lit up agreeably. "Oh much better but in view of all the travelling ahead of her tomorrow she decided to retire an hour ago. As for Reginald, well he's doing some ghastly paperwork in the study. So you see, I'm completely alone and eagerly awaiting news of your day."

There was much of interest to tell and despite an early start planned for the next day it was midnight when Kate finally bade her companion goodnight.

The following morning Dora and Kate said their farewells to Victoria and Reginald at the station. They barely had time for their carriage door to be opened and suitcases placed aboard when promptly at ten o'clock the train departed. They left behind a sky of nondescript grey with little promise of sunshine. Soon the engine gathered momentum and as it sped its way inland, belching thick, black smoke into the atmosphere, long flat stretches of marshland faded into the background.

Kate stared out of the carriage window. She found it hard to believe less than three weeks had passed by. Much had happened during the period to raise her spirits and it was incomprehensible now to think that on the outward journey, her association with Charles Jameson had seen her plummet to the depths of despair. But that was all in the past she mused and as the memory of his caress enveloped her, she regarded herself fortunate that fate had seen fit to reunite them.

"Are you all right Katherine?" The sound of Dora's voice dispersed her rambling thoughts and she smiled as she moved her gaze from the window and looked across at her companion.

"Oh yes, but forgive me Dora, it is I who should be enquiring after your health." Her deep brown eyes studied the older woman's features, " I pray that journeying so soon after your malaise will not upset you further," she added with a note of concern.

Dora shook her head encouragingly, " Indeed no child, I am fully back to strength," she replied with a determined air, " but then I was so looking forward to returning home that little would have deterred me."

Kate looked perplexed. "Do you not feel the benefit of your cousin's hospitality?" she queried softly.

"Oh indeed yes. I enjoyed my visit and have no wish to disparage my kin, they are good, generous folk," Dora insisted "but I wasn't built for a lengthy spell of cosseting. I must confess I'm anxious to return to the familiar hub of country life." Then, regretting her bluntness her homely face displayed misgivings, "Do you think me ungrateful Katherine?"

Satisfied nothing was untoward Kate relaxed at the query. "On the contrary," she laughed, leaning across the carriage and squeezing Dora's hand reassuringly, "the good doctor would no doubt be pleased to hear your words. I suspect he is eagerly awaiting your presence. Indeed you have much to return to."

"Yes Katherine I am a lucky woman," she stated philosophically, "Gerald is a kind and loving companion and absence has truly heightened my fondness for him. I hope that one day you will find such a partner."

Once again such openness tempted Kate to divulge her secret. But she had given Charles her word and in answer merely smiled assent. "I wonder how Albert has fared since our departure?" Kate queried tentatively, hoping to change the subject.

"No doubt Edwin will have kept him abreast of all the news," Dora replied. "Such a nice young man. He deserves a good woman," she concluded, scrutinizing Kate's features for a favourable response.

Kate nodded her head in agreement, though in truth, when her mind conjured up an image of Edwin and she dwelt on the matter, for some inexplicable reason she was irked by the possibility of another party intruding upon their friendship. Suddenly she experienced a certain empathy with Dora's wish to return to the tranquillity of the countryside. For as pleasurable as the holiday had been, she had to confess that a hectic social life would not be her choice on a permanent basis. Upon reflection it appeared a somewhat vacuous existence, with little enduring satisfaction to recommend it. Indeed, the more she considered the matter, the more eager she became to involve herself with duties at the farm. With a puzzled frown she returned her gaze to the window and pondered on the fact that marriage to Charles would change all that.

The previous day, upon his insistence, she had willingly cast aside plans for the future. Today however, the prospect of where they would make their home together became of paramount importance. She knew the cottage at Pembleton farm was meagre. And although a splendid family house could be built on the land adjacent, in truth, she could not picture Charles content in a backwater such as Hengleford.

Presently, exhausted by the previous day's excursion, Kate leaned back in her seat and closed her eyes Soon the monotonous motion of the swaying carriage lulled her into a fitful sleep. Despite the numerous stoppages en route, Kate remained oblivious to them all, until suddenly, Dora's voice rippled through the air and she felt her companion's hand upon her shoulder.

"Come Katherine, we are home," Dora exclaimed as she reached for the suitcases cradled in a mesh of twine above the seats of their compartment. There was a piercing whistle and screech of brakes as the train came to a standstill and a moment later, a porter on the platform opened the carriage door and the familiar sight of Gerald Parkins came forward to greet them.

"My dears, how good it is to see you," he exulted, pecking his wife's cheek and hugging her small, rounded frame. "Did you enjoy your stay?" He turned to Kate and his pale, blue eyes gleamed with satisfaction as he marvelled aloud at how well she looked. "Ah yes," he surmised, embracing her in a fatherly fashion. "The sea air has brought a glow to those cheeks. You undoubtedly feel the better for it eh?"

"Dear doctor," Kate laughed happily, "how nice it is to see you." Her enthusiasm was genuine, for it was good to see him and to be on home ground once more.

"Doubtless you both have much to tell," Gerald Parkins confirmed with a knowing smile.

Dora slipped her hand excitedly through his arm and as he extended his free arm towards Kate, they began to walk the length of the platform to the sound of his wife's excited chatter. A porter followed and after placing their suitcases in the car, they were soon wending their way through the heart warming familiarity of the Northamptonshire countryside. A short time later, when the gated entrance to the farm came into view, Kate experienced a mixture of relief and satisfaction at the sight of Albert leaning against it, puffing leisurely upon his pipe as he awaited their arrival.

In stature Albert was a spindly five foot two, with little hair beneath the chequered cap placed at a jaunty angle upon his head. Nonetheless, he was strong and capable and his small, open features and clean shaven face revealed an honesty that all respected.

Suddenly Kate was overwhelmed by an eagerness to resume her role, albeit a temporary one, as mistress of Pembleton farm.

Prompted by his wife's return, Gerald Parkins was in good spirits too and he tooted the horn in a frivolous fashion as he brought the car to a standstill.

"Afternoon Doctor, Mrs Parkins," Albert remarked, tipping his cap respectfully to the doctor and his wife as he walked towards them.

"Nice to see you back Mrs P." he grinned, springing forward to relieve Kate of her baggage with a zest that belied his sixty-seven years.

"It's good to be home Albert," Kate remarked happily. Then with a promise to visit Dora in the near future, she waved a cheery farewell to her companions and watched as they motored out of sight. "Has all gone well in my absence," she enquired eagerly, as Albert closed the gate behind them. "You must come in to the cottage for a cup of tea and give me all the news."

"Well, to tell you the truth it's my first day on the farm since Saturday. I got this cold on me chest and doctor made me stay a'bed."

A look of concern shrouded Kate's features. "Oh I am sorry to hear that Albert," she replied sympathetically. "Are you feeling better now?"

Albert nodded his head reassuringly. "It was lucky Master Edwin arrived when he did though."

"Edwin?" Kate queried.

"Aye," Albert remarked, lifting his cap and scratching the few wisps of greying hair beneath it. "He's been a seeing to things and would have been here now, but he took off in pony and trap on an errand in the village."

Together they approached the cottage and Albert stepped quickly in front of her to open the door. Perturbed by his news, Kate stepped gingerly over the threshold. About to barrage Albert with questions, she spied a fire flaring brightly in the fireplace and a vase of tall, stemmed roses placed neatly upon the clean, scrubbed table. It was a welcome sight. Though the cottage seemed smaller than ever after her spacious quarters at the Hamilton's premises, she took pleasure in the knowledge that however meagre, the property belonged to her utterly and completely. The smell of freshly baked bread drifted through the air and lingered pleasantly under her nose, reinforcing her positive thoughts.

Albert noted her look of pleasure and with a wry grin rested her baggage on the floor beside the dresser.

"That'll be Mr Edwin's doing," he rambled on happily, "he got young Ted's Ma to clean and bake special for your homecoming he did."

Kate was about to comment on Edwin's thoughtfulness when she heard the approach of pony and trap. Suddenly Edwin appeared in the doorway. The wind had dishevelled his streaky, blond hair into a boyish untidiness and his cheeks that bore a healthy outdoor complexion now heightened in colour at the sight of Kate.

He bound forward, his steady grey eyes gleaming with pleasure. "My dear Kate, how good it is to see you," he exulted, hugging her in a friendly fashion.

"Dear Edwin," she enthused, brushing her lips affectionately against the coolness of his face.

Then holding her at arm's length, Edwin scanned her features with a look of approval. "Why you look radiant. The sea air has certainly had the desired effect."

Kate's deep brown eyes softened at the compliment. How gratifying it was to set eyes upon her dear companion once more. In truth, amidst all the recent comings and goings she had forgotten what joy there was to be had in his presence. Her lips parted in a generous smile and with the slightest of curtsies she remarked teasingly, "Your words as always are most heartening kind sir."

They made a handsome couple Albert surmised as he sucked thoughtfully on the stem of his pipe. If Mistress has any sense she'd encourage that one, worth his salt he was. Not like some. Having concluded his observation, he had no wish to intrude upon their reunion and anxious to be off coughed loudly.

Kate glanced over Edwin's shoulder at her foreman. "Oh forgive me for keeping you waiting, Albert," she remarked apologetically. "You haven't yet had the tea I promised."

"Don't fret none. The Missus will have one ready when I get home." Without further ado he moved towards the door and on reaching it turned. "It's good to see you looking so well. Now don't go rushing up at the crack of dawn," he chided, with a wag of his finger. "I'll be seeing to things as usual in the morning." He tipped his cap respectfully, "Mr Edwin."

"Albert." Edwin nodded with a smile, "thank you again for all your advice."

The door closed with a thud, leaving an awkward silence. Suddenly, in unison, Kate and Edwin started to speak.

"After you," Edwin gestured politely.

"No, please you..."

For a moment they eyed each other in a comical fashion, then, as their friendship found that old familiar footing, the sound of their laughter rippled through the air.

"Now," retorted Edwin masterfully, moving further into the kitchen to make tea and promptly returning with a loaded tray. "Take off your coat and be settled at the table Kate. I shall pour whilst you give me all your news."

Daylight faded and some hours later they were still engrossed in conversation. "The extra few days were well spent, I trust," Edwin queried as he knelt to place a fresh log upon the open fire.

Kate pondered momentarily on telling him of her encounter with his brother. If she did not, he would most certainly think it remiss of her when Charles spoke of it. Yes we all spent an eventful weekend with the Clitheroe's in the country. Oh, and by the merest of coincidences your brother Charles was there." she added the latter as if it were an afterthought.

Edwin did not seem unduly perturbed. "Ah, so you met Annabel."

"Annabel?" Kate echoed.

"Charles's fiancée, he spoke of his intention some weeks ago."

Kate's colour drained and for a moment she could find no words with which to reply.

Unaware of the impact of his remark, Edwin had moved across the room into the kitchen to wash his hands at the sink. "Well?" he continued innocently. "What was your opinion of, and I quote, the vision of loveliness."

Kate stared at the breadth of Edwin's back through the kitchen doorway, her mind in turmoil. Anxious that her companion should remain in ignorance of her dilemma, she sprang from her chair and opened her baggage, searching frantically for the memento she had purchased for him. "I did not see the fiancée you speak of," she replied calmly.

"No matter." Edwin shrugged, drying his hands vigorously on a nearby towel, "my brother's amours are of little consequence. And now, having related all news of Pembleton farm and gathered in details of your holiday, I have something of interest of my own to tell. There is a property at Malsor I would like you to see." He looked at her directly with a broad grin upon his face and at any other time Kate would have been enthusiastic on her companion's account. Now however, questions and answers concerning Charles invaded her thoughts and in all honesty she paid little attention to what Edwin was saying.

"The site is perfect," he continued excitedly, "not too far from Hengleford, on the ..." His voice trailed into oblivion as he noted Kate's glazed expression. "Kate?" he quizzed.

Kate's thoughts dispersed in a haze of uncertainty. "I'm sorry Edwin, where was the property?"

Misinterpreting her lack of interest as a sign of weariness, Edwin rose from his chair. "It is I who should apologise, for the hour is late and you must be exhausted from your journey." He took her hands into his own and squeezed them lightly. "Perhaps I could call upon you tomorrow afternoon to discuss the matter further."

"Would you?" Kate commented encouragingly.

"It will be my pleasure," he remarked softly, bending forward to kiss her lightly upon the cheek. "Sleep well and remember Albert's instruction. Don't rush up at crack of dawn," he mimicked.

Despite Kate's smile of amusement Edwin's departure prompted a certain relief. After bolting the door behind him, she returned to her chair beside the fire to ruminate upon the news of Charles's fiancée.

Could Edwin have misunderstood his brother? Had Charles really intended to marry another? Perhaps, and then when she herself had appeared on the scene, he had discarded such thoughts. For a moment her outlook brightened and she wished now that she had enquired more of this Annabel. Leaning forward upon her chair she reached for the poker and prodded the embers of the fire in an aimless fashion. Inevitably, like the flowing and ebbing of the tide doubts returned to taunt her subconscious. Slowly she reflected upon her lover's behaviour the previous day. She relived every word, every gesture he had made and in her heart of hearts she knew the latter explanation was unlikely. After all, was it not Charles himself who had suggested their plans be kept secret. Was it really necessary, unless of course he had intended all along to exit from her life once the day was over. Had he no scruples; had she no shame. How could she have been so naïve. There was to be no engagement ring, no wedding, it had all been a cruel charade. Disappointment overwhelmed her and as the truth of the matter dawned she began to weep uncontrollably.

By midnight the warm glow of the fire had petered into paper grey ashes. And as her tears subsided, Kate turned off the lamps about the room and made her way wearily up the narrow staircase to her bed. It was not the first time she had encountered a restless night on Charles Jameson's behalf and though he had deceived her with all the skill and expertise of a libertine, to make matters worse she could no longer find excuses for her own behaviour.

In a juvenile fashion she had longed for a romantic reunion and in truth, from the moment she had set eyes upon him again her passion had been all consuming, over-ruling any effort at common sense.

He had no intention of keeping his word, of that she was now convinced. Somehow, somehow she must cast him from her mind forever and begin life anew.

Chapter Six

It was after seven o'clock the following morning when Kate finally awoke and dressed. Still tired from a restless sleep, she stood at the bedroom window and pulling back the curtains observed the grey, dark October morning with a philosophical air. From the yard below she could hear Ted's chirpy whistle coming from the milking shed and she saw the outline of Albert disappearing into the newly extended winter quarters for the herd. Such normality would prove to be her saving grace, for despite all that had happened there was work to be done, with no time to linger upon her past indiscretions. Nonetheless, on scanning the woods to the left she felt a pang of regret, for it was there she had experienced her first passionate encounter with Charles. With a heartfelt sigh she thrust the moment of recall into the depths of her subconscious and as her eyes followed the line of oak trees on the distant horizon, a sense of achievement overcame her momentary lapse of despair. As far as the eye could see the land belonged to her. She had endured much to reach this eventuality and now, whatever befell, would devote her time to it.

After a scanty breakfast she unpacked her baggage from the previous day and checked her larder for food. Fortunately Ted's mother had seen fit to furnish it with adequate supplies and she made a mental note to ride into the village later to repay her for her kindness.

Later, donning her boots and an old thick winter coat, she stepped outside into the cold damp air to inspect the barn and livestock.

Young Ted, who was still busy cleaning out the stalls, was pleased at her appearance and promptly approached her with new ideas for the storage of winter feed. Kate was impressed by his forward thinking and on return to the cottage to attend to the accounts, decided that both he and Albert warranted more by way of a weekly wage. She would discuss the matter with Edwin when he next paid a visit, after all, he was fair minded in such things and always to be relied upon for advice.

Her thoughts lingered pleasantly upon Edwin as she sat at the table with her book-work spread about. Indeed, whilst others were not what they appeared, he remained the same, a veritable tower of strength. The highs and lows she had undergone with Charles had left her mentally and physically drained, only now did she fully appreciate the true value of such a friend. Much to her surprise Edwin called upon her at midday, somewhat earlier than expected, but, as he readily explained, an urgent message requesting his presence in London by nine o'clock the following morning, meant he had to depart Hengleford later that very day.

After preparing a lunch of cold ham, potato's and the inevitable pot of tea, they sat together at the table and talked at length of the farm hands wages and Edwin's proposed cottage.

"I must confess I am considering changes of my own Edwin," Kate remarked thoughtfully.

"Oh?" Edwin's eyebrows arched with the query as he reached for the jar of pickles.

"Would I have sufficient funds to build a large house here on the farm?" she asked, refilling his empty teacup and placing it by his side.

"Heavens yes, without a doubt. I must bring a copy of your portfolio from chambers so that you may see for yourself the extent of your investments."

"Then I could begin to enquire after a reputable builder?" she remarked cautiously.

"Well first you require a surveyor to examine the site you have in mind, then an architect to design the property and lastly a builder you can trust to do the work." Edwin looked at her directly, "But I have another suggestion. Why do we not build a house together you and I? I am under no false illusion that you love me Kate, but perhaps in time." His voice trailed off into oblivion and though his face revealed nothing, Kate sensed an underlying anticipation as he awaited her answer.

Her voice mellowed. "But the farm means a great deal to me now Edwin. I could not entertain the prospect of giving it up. I..."

"No need," he interrupted quickly. "I am aware of how proud you must be of your achievements here over the last few months. I would not dream of suggesting otherwise. Indeed, if we were to marry I would be working in the city for much of the week and would not wish to interfere with your commitments here." Having sped over his proposal Edwin's face broke into a sheepish grin. "I know, I promised not to speak of marriage again," he continued apologetically, "truth is Kate, I find myself at a loss without you." His steady grey eyes stared into hers, exposing a vulnerability that caught Kate unawares.

"Dear Edwin," she replied softly, leaning across the table to place her hand over his, "I do treasure our time

124

together and have come to rely solely upon your good judgement."

"Then have we not a sound basis upon which to build a life together?" he urged.

Kate paused to reflect upon his words for there was a deal of truth in what he said.

Edwin noted her hesitation and was heartened by it. "Say no more until I return on Friday my dear," he murmured, giving her hand an affectionate squeeze. "And now," he continued, rising from his chair, " I must be off. Landlord Simms is stocktaking of all things and I promised him some assistance before I left."

Kate eyed him fondly and upon his departure assured him she would give his proposal a great deal of thought.

Exactly three days later, Kate was aware that she had missed her menstrual cycle and the fact disturbed her greatly, for such womanly occurrences were usually as regular as clockwork. Her mind erupted into a maze of hypothesis. Having been betrayed by a philanderer was she now to be beset by a new quandary? Her blood ran cold. Was there a further price to pay for her naivety? Over the last few months she had gained respect from the nearby community, but should a child result from her irresponsible devotion to Charles Jameson her name would be bandied about the village like some common harlot. She would become an outcast and such humiliation would be hard to bear. A child. Was it likely? Was it possible? Her stomach contracted and as panic gripped her, her thoughts turned blindly to Edwin's proposal of marriage. What could she say to this gentle man who adored her so. Dare she confess her fears and risk losing her dearest friend, or might she accept his offer and leave him in ignorance of her personal anguish. The latter was indeed a tempting solution.

Numerous tasks enveloped her throughout the day and it was late when Kate eventually retired to her bed. Nevertheless, she had collected her thoughts sufficient to despise herself for even having considered such skulduggery with regard to Edwin. He was a trusted companion and worthy of better treatment. No. If time confirmed her suspicions she would seek advice from Gerald Parkins. Whatever his personal opinion of her, a child's welfare would be his uppermost concern.

Despite the short lapse of her period, in a most peculiar way she was somewhat in awe of such a possibility. A baby. Are prospective mother's intuitive about such things she wondered.

The following morning Kate arose early and with the determined air of her former self, cast all supposition from the previous day aside. There was, she concluded, little point in worrying about such an event before fact deemed it necessary and it would be unwise of her to assume that a child should result from the lack of one period. With a lighter heart she proceeded to clean the kitchen floor and to all intents and purposes, planned to prepare pony and trap for a ride into the village later. Soon after ten o'clock however, Edwin called at the cottage.

His visit caught Kate completely by surprise, for he was not due to arrive at Hengleford until the following day. Dressed in a dark, worsted overcoat, with collar upturned for protection against the coolness of the October morning, he beamed openly as he crossed the threshold and picked his way carefully over the wet stone floor.

"Forgive me for calling at such an inconvenient time my dear, but I have news to relate that I could contain no longer." A merry twinkle infiltrated his grey eyes and Kate was at once intrigued by his excited manner. With a smile of welcome she placed her mop and bucket into the corner of the room and began to dry her hands in the folds of her apron.

"No matter Edwin, pray be seated and tell me your news whilst I make a pot of tea," she remarked genially, moving through the doorway into the kitchen.

Ignoring the offer of a chair Edwin traced her footsteps and hovered restlessly behind her. "I have been invited to attend a conference in Paris at ten o'clock on Friday, November the twenty-ninth," he blurted. "It concerns changes afoot regarding legal matters and the speaker is a well-respected barrister."

"Paris," Kate reiterated with a modicum of disbelief.

"Mmm," he acknowledged. A boyish smugness crossed his angular features and as Kate turned to face him she warmed affectionately to his mood.

"Well your fondness for art and the like will certainly be gratified by such a visit. How I envy you," she sighed.

Edwin studied her face intently. "Then marry me Kate and accompany me on the trip."

Kate caught her breath. "But I...I..."

"The conference is merely a one day formality," he continued quickly, "but I have taken the liberty of arranging a lengthy absence from chambers before the date specified. A special licence would not be impossible to obtain and we could spend our honeymoon in one of the most romantic cities in the world."

Kate's deep brown eyes grew wide at his persistence. "But Edwin, I have just returned from a holiday. I could hardly expect Albert to..."

"Albert would be only too delighted to take charge," he interrupted eagerly, "if only to make amends for his absence on the last occasion. And should he require assistance then extra hands are readily available in the village. Rest assured, I would see to it they were well taken care of financially."

"I can see that you have given the matter a great deal of thought," Kate remarked, pursing her lips attractively in a knowing smile.

"My dear Kate," Edwin enthused, moving closer and resting his hands upon her shoulders, "I have such plans for us! A splendid honeymoon, a house to be built at a location of your choosing, a re-arrangement of my chambers in the city so that I will not hinder you whilst you are fully occupied here. Oh my dear, the future could hold so much for us together. Please, please I beg you, allow me to share the burden of your responsibilities. Say yes, and I swear you will never have cause for regret."

Faced with such devotion it was difficult for Kate to remain impassive. Indeed, even as Edwin spoke she found herself being swept away on the crest of his enthusiasm. Would it not be unkind to dampen and deflate such ardour. Her conscience taunted.

She sensed intuitively that this was an ultimatum. For Edwin was a proud man and would not demean himself to ask again at a later date. Her mind was in turmoil, for in the past he had proved a reliable rock upon which she could lean, a loyal confidante. She had no wish to jeopardize this alliance, or for that matter, remain alone for the rest of her days. And yet, without disclosing her past indiscretion their relationship could go no further.

With a deep breath she gathered strength for the moment of truth. "Edwin," she began softly, lowering her gaze to the floor, "before I give my answer I have a matter to speak of with regard to your brother." Would he insist upon details? Enquire further into events? The loss of his companionship was a perilous consequence.

Edwin placed his hand beneath her chin and raised her head gently to meet his steady gaze. "I have only one question Kate. Do you care for me?" he emphasized.

Kate's features relaxed at the query and at once her deep brown eyes softened with obvious affection. "My dear, you know that to be true, but..."

"Then what is past is past, over and done. And now my dear, please give me your answer," he stated earnestly.

Although Kate's confession had fallen far short of its entirety, the attempt on her part to begin it salved her troubled mind. Indeed, all she could think of was that at this moment in time, Edwin offered her the protection of his name and freedom to continue to run the farm as she wished. Why then should she throw away a chance of real happiness for the sake of intuition, a possibility of an event that may never come to pass.

"Then yes Edwin, oh yes my dear," she concluded, taking pleasure in the look of relief upon her companion's face as he gathered her into his arms. They met as equals, devoted to each other's wellbeing and when his lips touched Kate's in a tender, almost reverential fashion, the blinding adoration she had felt for Charles Jameson seemed a lifetime since.

When Edwin finally released her from his embrace, his exuberance was clear to see. "Come Kate," he urged, taking her by the hand and edging towards the door, "put on your hat and coat. We will drive into the village and give the news to Dora and Gerald."

"But the chores are unfinished," Kate chided lightly, pointing to the bucket in the corner of the room. "As for my dress," her delicate features puckered with distaste as she fingered her work attire, "it is quite unsuitable for a trip into the village."

Beguiled by her femininity Edwin laughed good heartedly. "Then away with you and change. I'll attend to the floor in your absence." And before she could comment further, he had removed his overcoat and jacket and rolled up the sleeves of his immaculate white shirt. The gesture prompted a touching response from Kate and as she climbed the steep stairs to her bedroom, she ruminated upon Edwin's willingness to tackle any task. In hindsight it was a most endearing attribute and without doubt, one which had boosted his popularity so readily amongst the locals.

Suddenly an unexpected image of Charles cast misgivings upon her decision to marry. Had she accepted Edwin's proposal too readily. Would the memory of those bittersweet liaisons with his brother forever haunt her? A comparison of the two men battled away in her mind as she dressed, although thankfully, by the time she had made ready for the journey into the village, her genuine affection for Edwin dismissed any further wavering. Indeed, whatever the future held, the burden of her indiscretion was hers and hers alone. She had no wish to cause Edwin unnecessary anguish and would willingly devote her time to making him happy.

When Kate finally reappeared both mop and bucket were out of sight and the large peg rug, freshly shaken, was stretched out before the open fireplace. Edwin was about to put on his jacket, but he paused in the task as Kate entered the room and at sight of her his heartbeat quickened. Despite wedlock to that scoundrel Pembleton, her soft brown eyes and delicate features bore a remarkable quality of innocence he mused. Indeed, in her cream high necked blouson and lengthy brown skirt she looked so delightfully fresh and nubile that he was overwhelmed by a feeling of tenderness towards her. In truth, he had admired her ever since their first encounter. Had it not been so he would not have risked the possibility of a second rebuff.

Kate gave him a tantalizing smile as she pirouetted before him. "Well Edwin, am I not more suitably attired now?" she questioned teasingly.

Her companion's face glowed with pleasure. He had offered an opinion on many matters in the past, but none so intimate. It was a simple request but it moved him deeply and in silence he deliberated upon his good fortune.

"There is some doubt?" Kate queried softly, her words breaking through his reverie. Her eyes clouded somewhat as they searched his for confirmation.

At once Edwin shook his head. "None my precious Kate," he said, moving towards her with arms out-stretched. "In truth, I fear I shall have to guard you most diligently in Paris, for you will be sure to turn every man's head."

From many the words would have sounded trite and insincere, but from Edwin, who as a rule had little time for flattery and inconsequential remarks, it was praise indeed. She sighed contentedly as he swept her into his arms to give her an affectionate hug. After some discussion, Kate put on her hat and coat and they drove into the village.

There was a chill in the air but the wind had mellowed and though the countryside was stripped bare of autumnal colour, the sun appeared from a pale blue sky, as if to acknowledge the couples happiness. The journey was but a short distance, yet so leisurely was the trip that it was almost noon when they rang the doorbell of the doctor's imposing ivy covered house. As luck would have it Gerald Parkins and his wife were both at home, though alas, as the elated couple followed Dora across the hall and entered the parlour, they noted a table set for lunch.

"I must apologise for this untimely interruption," Edwin began, "it is my fault I assure you. It's simply that Kate and I have news that would not keep," he concluded, placing his arm protectively about Kate's shoulders. When he proudly revealed the glad tidings, their hosts were delighted and congratulated them in unison. Indeed, if Kate had been their daughter they could not have been more pleased or chosen a more worthy partner than Edwin.

"It may be a little early in the day," winked the cheery doctor, "but this calls for a glass of Madeira, eh Dora?"

"Oh indeed," confirmed his excited wife, promptly moving to the cupboard for glasses. "Now sit yourselves down, the pair of you and take a little lunch with us."

Soon after the toast the men began a conversation with regard to the new fifteen horse powered car that the manufacturers Austin had just revealed to the public. Despite Dora's insistence to the contrary, Kate followed her into the kitchen to help prepare extra food for the table. "I am delighted with your news Katherine," Dora enthused as they entered the large comfortable kitchen.

A smile tweaked the corners of Kate's lips as she watched her companion slicing generous portions of beef and placing them on a large platter. "I suspected you might be, though I must confess it has taken me somewhat by surprise. There is so little time to arrange things."

Dora looked up from her task. "My dear girl, you know that I am ready to help you both in any way that I can."

Kate nodded her head gratefully. "I must first dispatch an invitation to Victoria and Reginald. I value their friendship also and wish to seek advice from Victoria on the matter of a suitable trousseau for the trip to Paris."

"Then extend the invitation to include a few days stay with Gerald and myself," Dora remarked. "That should allow you and Victoria ample time to spend in London in search of a new wardrobe."

"Oh, may I Dora?" I must confess the farm is far from adequate for their needs." Her voice trailed into oblivion as a hundred and one things crowded her mind.

"Ah now, since you have mentioned it," Dora exclaimed, " might I ask where you have decided to live until the new house Edwin spoke of is being built?"

A perplexed look crossed Kate's features as she reached for the cutlery. "Truly Dora, all is moving so swiftly we have had little time to discuss the matter."

"Well if there is any difficulty, Gerald and I would be only too pleased to accommodate you both on your return from Paris."

Kate's features relaxed and she looked upon her companion fondly. "Bless you Dora."

"Have a word with Edwin when you are alone," Dora broke in, "after all he may have other plans."

"Whatever is decided the offer is a generous one and I thank you from the bottom of my heart," Kate replied softly, stepping forward to give her mentor the gentlest of hugs.

Touched by the rareness of the moment, Dora's plump cheeks flushed with colour and tears of joy welled up in her eyes. "Praise be girl, 'tis the least we can do. Now fill the kettle and we'll make a pot of tea for the table," she concluded, lifting the corner of her apron to wipe a tear from her cheek.

It was mid afternoon when Edwin and Kate took their leave and returned to the cottage. Whilst Edwin busied himself stoking up the fire a conversation began as to other invitations that needed to be dispatched with haste.

"I know so little of your life in London, Edwin," Kate hesitated, reluctant at first to make reference to his family, nonetheless the query had to be made. "Have you friends or relatives you might wish to invite?" she asked, looking up from the kitchen table where she sat with writing paper and pen at the ready.

Edwin pursed his lips and with a determined air shook his head. "I've numerous acquaintances though none I would wish to take part in a social event. As for family, Charles is my only remaining relative and at present fully occupied with plans of his own. I doubt he will find time to make an appearance," he replied, setting the question at rest. The truth of it was, Edwin had no desire to inform Charles of their arrangements until it was absolutely necessary, indeed, for the moment he was anxious to avoid further conversation on the matter, for the mere mention of his brother's name made him uneasy.

Kate sensed his reluctance. Though there was little daylight left, she took him by the hand and insisted they walk the meadow together before dark, to search out common ground, a site agreeable to them both where their house should be built. That at least would be one decision less before they parted company that evening.

Despite the long weekend ahead of them time passed swiftly. Whilst Edwin visited reputable builders in the area, Kate attended to chores about the farm. Later she sought out the necessary documents Edwin required to take back with him on return to London.

At midday on Monday, Edwin telephoned Dora from London with news that after much debate with various authorities, he had obtained a grant for a special licence. The wedding was to take place at the registry office close to his chambers on Friday the eighth of November at ten forty-five in the morning.

"Well done Edwin," Dora enthused, "I will give Katherine the news when she visits this afternoon."

"And," Edwin continued cheerfully, "by way of a thank you for all your support, I have arranged for you, Gerald and Mr and Mrs Hamilton to stay two nights at the Royal. That is on Thursday the seventh and Friday the eighth of November, whereupon we shall all return to the hotel after the wedding ceremony for a private reception. I hasten to add that the cost will be charged to my account."

Dora gasped with surprise at the latter.

"Have I been too presumptuous?" Edwin queried with concern.

"Of course not, Edwin," Dora replied perkily, anxious to alleviate any doubts, "but I had no idea that we were to..." she broke off somewhat hesitant in case of misunderstanding his intention.

"Dear me, Dora," Edwin interrupted apologetically, "had I forgotten in all the excitement to ask if you and

Gerald would oblige us by taking part in the ceremonies. I understand Kate has already dispatched a similar request to the Hamiltons, with news of the actual date to follow."

"No matter," Dora chuckled, "I'll take it upon myself to answer for all we shall be honoured to play such an active role in sharing your day my dear." At that moment the bell on the surgery door rang loudly. "I must go Edwin. Gerald is out at present and someone is at the door."

"I understand. My best wishes to all and I look forward to seeing you at the weekend. Goodbye."

With her wedding day less than three weeks away there was much to be done and from the onset Kate was happy to leave arrangements for celebrations at the village hall in Dora's capable hands. Farm work, cattle feed, market transactions all had to be arranged with Albert, although as Edwin had predicted earlier, her foreman was only too pleased to learn he was to be left in charge to get on with the job. It was, as Albert put it, his personal contribution to the proceedings. In truth though, he was cheered by the news of Kate's forthcoming marriage to Edwin. To his mind the couple were well matched. "As for Mrs P," he declared to all and sundry whilst supping his ale in the Coach and Horses, "she has always been good to me and deserves a better goings on that she had with old Jack." The feeling amongst the locals was unanimous and the latter having been spoken aloud by Albert, quickly silenced anything untoward about Jack Pembleton having been buried so short a time.

On the fourteenth of October, the Hamilton's arrived at Hengleford for their short stay with Dora and Gerald.

Edwin motored from London especially for the occasion. Over a celebratory dinner at the doctor's house, it was apparent to all that Victoria approved of Katherine's intended. So much so that after dinner, when Gerald Parkins suggested the menfolk take in a little fresh air and exercise and the ladies were left to their own devices, Victoria confirmed her observations of Edwin aloud.

"You are a fortunate young woman Katherine. Edwin has a steady gaze and open manner which indicates to me a trustworthy individual. Were that his brother was half the man," she concluded thoughtfully. Kate's cheeks flooded with colour at the unexpected reference to Charles and as she collected dishes from the table and made to follow Dora into the kitchen, her hands began to tremble. Victoria, observant as ever, rose from her chair and touched Kate's arm lightly. "I suspect that you too were once distracted by that rascal's charms eh Katherine?" she prompted. Her bright, blue eyes stared directly into Kate's and for a moment Kate felt that her companion was aware of all that had gone before. Indeed, if she did not know, a sudden urge to confess all overwhelmed her. She knew that the matter would go no further and the unloading of such a burden would relieve her greatly. Nonetheless, the shame of it prevented her and she dare not. "No matter my dear," Victoria continued, dismissing Kate's obvious embarrassment with a shrug of her shoulders, "you have chosen wisely. As for our gallivanting Charles, well, he has taken on a little more than he can cope with at present. His fiancée, pretty young Annabel Soames, is keeping a very tight rein upon him I hear."

"Their wedding is to take place shortly after ours I understand," Kate echoed, somewhat surprised by her own composure.

"Mmm," Victoria nodded, "and a glamorous affair it will be if Annabel's mother has her way. But then the family is fabulously rich my dear and Annabel is their only daughter. But tut, you and I have far more important topics to discuss."

With time at a premium, arrangements were made by telephone for an overnight stay in London the following day, specifically for the purpose of selecting Kate's trousseau. Dora declined the offer to accompany them as she already had much to plan for the forthcoming event and in truth would have felt something of an encumbrance in the unfamiliar opulence of London's fashion houses. A short time later, somewhat chilled by the night air, the men re-appeared, and as it was almost ten o'clock, Edwin suggested it was time he escorted Kate back to Pembleton farm. Before leaving the group, he made his apologies to the ladies for being unable to drive them personally to London; an early appointment with an important client deemed it necessary for him to leave his lodgings at the crack of dawn. So, after seeing Kate safely inside the cottage and making sure that all was well, he returned to the Coach and Horses for a much needed rest.

Shortly after Edwin's departure, Kate also retired to her bed. The day had been a full one and as she had spent so little of it at the farm, she too must rise early in an attempt to make amends. Once in bed however, sleep eluded her. Thoughts of the past and future intermingled and she lay awake procrastinating. There had been no time at all of late to reflect upon her decision to marry and in hindsight it would seem that she had been swept along by the joyous reaction of others. Now, as the wedding date drew nearer, the knowing of it had a sobering effect upon her earlier elation. Alone, in the quiet of her bedroom, niggling doubts began to gnaw at her subconscious. Had she ultimately chosen the road of deceit by not fully disclosing all her doubts to Edwin? Her menstrual cycle still had not shown itself, though in truth there had been no other sign of change in her physical condition. Were that she could turn back the clock and obliterate her last encounter with Charles Jameson. So her mind continued its familiar battle until eventually, drained of energy to pursue her problems any further, Kate fell into an exhausted sleep.

CHAPTER SEVEN

For Edwin, the drive back to chambers in the early hours was a pleasant experience. He encountered little in the way of traffic, which was doubly fortunate as his mind tended to wander in the preoccupation of future events. From time to time he pondered unwillingly upon Kate's openness with regard to his brother. In truth, he had no wish for her to enlarge upon the matter though it was obvious from her manner she had experienced a certain infatuation for Charles when he had called upon the Pembletons earlier in the year. But then, goodness knows, women worldlier than Kate had been taken in by his charm. Drawing comfort from the fact that she appeared content and had made no reference to his brother since that time, he put the matter to rest.

As he approached the suburbs of the metropolis, with the October sunshine glinting through the windows of the vehicle, he concluded it would now be prudent to inform Charles of his own wedding plans. Indeed, spurred on by good intentions he was already seated at his desk in chambers by eight o'clock and scanning the paperwork that had lain in wait for his perusal. At precisely nine o'clock Miss Bartholomew tapped his door and informed him Mr Bonham Spence had arrived and was seated in the waiting room. Sliding a comfortable chair across the carpet to rest opposite his own, Edwin asked her to show him in.

After the usual pleasantries he removed the necessary file from the left hand drawer of his desk and placed the documents awaiting his client's signature on the leather bound blotter in front of him. Time passed quickly as they discussed the paperwork in detail and soon, with business complete, the elderly bewhiskered Mr Bonham Spence rose to his feet to shake Edwin's hand in gratitude.

"I am indebted to you young man. Now, whatever befalls I have the satisfaction of knowing that all the legalities are in place." His grateful smile was tempered by the discomfort of arthritic limbs as he shuffled in a painful manner towards the exit. With a degree of concern for the disability of his client, Edwin stepped forward to open the door and on closing it returned to his desk and proceeded to study the pile of documents requiring his attention.

Promptly at ten o'clock Miss Bartholomew tapped his door and entered carrying the habitual pot of coffee and biscuits. Glancing up from his desk Edwin nodded to his secretary in a friendly manner. "Ah Miss Bartholomew, would you arrange for Mr Peabody to place these documents in the appropriate deed boxes?" he asked, waiting until she had set the refreshment tray down upon his desk before depositing them in her care.

"Mr Peabody has just left the premises to deliver an urgent letter to a client Mr Edwin, but he should be back shortly. I'll see that the task is done," she concluded efficiently.

"Oh, and has Mr Charles arrived yet?" Edwin enquired as she turned to leave.

Before she could answer his brother, looking somewhat subdued, appeared in the doorway. Edwin smiled amiably in his direction. "Have you a moment Charles?"

"Providing I am not to be hauled over the coals for one reason or another my time is yours," his brother replied, transmitting a winning smile to the bespectacled Miss Bartholomew, before moving forward and seating himself wearily in the leather wing chair opposite Edwin.

Edwin eyed him briefly with a modicum of concern, then studying the back of his departing secretary remarked. "Bring another cup would you Miss Bartholomew?"

She turned, nodded politely and after moving out of earshot, he returned his gaze to Charles. "Are you all right?"

Charles sighed dejectedly. "I fear not. The formalities of impending wedlock have dampened my spirits dear brother. You see before you," he continued with true thespian drama, "a man now denied of many bountiful pleasures." Whereupon he shifted restlessly in his seat and pointed an accusing finger at Edwin. "You are truly wise to avoid such a fate." His handsome features bore a crestfallen look as Miss Bartholomew re-entered, poured their coffee and quietly left the room.

Edwin's lips twisted in a wry smile. Annabel appeared to have curtailed his brother's freedom at an early stage. "As a matter of fact," he stated, "it is wedding arrangements I wish to speak of."

"Details evade me at present, but you are invited of course," Charles announced in a monotonous tone. "Though why anyone would care to witness such a spectacle is beyond my comprehension.

Edwin laughed aloud at his brother's sombre manner. "Come now, I understood your betrothed to be a charming girl. You are a lucky fellow by all accounts, but then it is not your wedding arrangements I wish to discuss, it is my own."

Charles spluttered into his coffee cup at the news. "YOU. Getting married?" he uttered in disbelief, placing his cup and saucer upon the tray on the desk and taking a large white handkerchief from the top pocket of his jacket. Suddenly his blue eyes took on an awareness that had been lacking and he leaned forward in his chair. "And who may I ask, is the fortunate lady?"

"Katherine Pembleton," Edwin replied, watching his brother's reaction closely.

Charles's manner showed nothing untoward as he rose from his chair, extended his hand and offered his most sincere congratulations. In truth however, he received the announcement with a mixture of envy and relief. For whilst Katherine's naivety had never failed to whet his lusty appetite, ever since their last rendezvous he had feared the possibility of a confrontation. Edwin's news was gratifying to say the least for any hint of unpleasantness would have ruined his chances of marrying into the wealthy Soames family. "Dismiss my pessimistic ramblings of earlier from your mind," Charles stated jovially. "I shall attend your wedding in full regalia."

"Unfortunately you will not," Edwin continued dryly as he searched amongst the papers on his desk. "One of us must visit and bring our files up-to-date on the Jaffer's estate in Scotland."

"What, that old crochet!" Charles retorted.

"Do not be hasty brother. The undertaking will be especially rewarding and help to keep you in the manner to which you have become accustomed over the years," Edwin remarked, moving the appropriate bundle of paperwork over the desk towards Charles.

"Could we not delay the inventory?" Charles argued persuasively.

"No unfortunately. Cecil Jaffers will be leaving the country on the first of December to spend the winter in warmer climes," Edwin stated calmly. "You would not wish me to delay my own wedding to accommodate him would you brother?"

"Ah, I see your predicament," Charles conceded. "Well in that case I shall go to the frozen wastes knowing that my frightful task will have served a good purpose. As for today, I have an engagement at eleven-thirty that will keep me busy for an hour, after which I shall take you out to lunch to celebrate your good fortune."

Suddenly a feeling of euphoria swept over Edwin and he smiled contentedly as he watched his brother rise and move briskly to the door. "My news appears to have lifted you out of the doldrums," he commented light-heartedly.

Charles hesitated at the threshold and glancing over his shoulder grinned in a mischievous fashion. "It is the knowledge that I tread the treacherous path of matrimony in good company brother," he quipped.

Edwin responded with a smile of amusement and after his brother had departed continued to sift through the remaining paperwork upon his desk.

True to his word Charles reappeared shortly after half past twelve and in a mood tantamount to secrecy ushered Edwin into a waiting taxi. The weather that had appeared so promising earlier had changed for the worse and as ominous dark clouds hovered overhead, a light shower of sleet began to fall. By the time they reached their destination the temperature had dropped and a white film of snow covered the pavements. For wintry conditions to arrive before the autumn was barely over was indeed an unusual occurrence.

For Edwin the cosy French restaurant some distance from the noise of the city proved a pleasant surprise. All too familiar with the lavish tastes of his brother he had feared a more opulent eating place. Indeed, as he sat in his chair sipping leisurely at his aperitif, the convivial atmosphere of the restaurant lulled him into a sense of wellbeing.

From across the table Charles studied his brother's relaxed features. "Knowing your dislike of ostentatious places I thought you might like it here," he commented good-humouredly.

Edwin smiled approvingly and encouraged by his brother's thoughtfulness began to give a more detailed account of his future plans.

For all concerned, the days that followed appeared totally consumed with arrangements of one kind or another. In Hengleford, Dora, with the aid of several local ladies, had set in motion arrangements for a magnificent buffet to take place in the village hall on the evening of Saturday the second of November. All were given specific tasks for the making of sandwiches, cooked meats and pies, as well as an inspiring variety of mouth-watering cakes. And since all from the neighbourhood would be attending the festivities, a decision to close the Inn for a few hours was suggested by Landlord Simms, who would then be free to transfer barrels of beer and other refreshments to serve at the venue. For entertainment, Tom Barratt, Albert's young nephew, who was always in demand for parties such as this, was to play his accordion, thereby supplying the music for any singing or dancing that took place.

Dora was amazed by the zeal shown by those taking up the various tasks, though later she discovered from exchanges overheard in the village that it was their high regard for Kate and Edwin that had spurred them on. After the evening's celebrations Edwin would be staying overnight at the Coach and Horses. Following a late breakfast, he would drive to his chambers on Sunday the third of November to finish off any necessary paperwork and arrangements. On Monday he would discuss with Miss Bartholomew matters regarding recent queries from clients and to inform her to summon Mr Peabody's help should she find herself in difficulty. Edwin had every confidence that together, his long standing secretary and trustworthy clerk, could between them solve any problem that might occur. But should an extreme emergency arise, he also gave her the telephone number of the Inn where Charles would be staying, which was in close proximity to the Jaffer's estate in Scotland. They could then explain their predicament and Charles would either hold the matter in abeyance until his return or suggest a colleague from chambers nearby to assist.

By Tuesday the fifth of November he had packed his trunk which was to be collected from his apartment that morning and delivered to the Royal to await his arrival on Thursday. On Wednesday, with an overnight bag full to capacity and all his tasks complete, he set out for Hengleford to be in place for the collection of his bride to be and to deliver her and her entourage, complete with trousseau to the Royal Hotel in London the following morning. Reginald Hamilton was to assist by following in his own vehicle with luggage and the remainder of the wedding party. Edwin was looking forward to this particular journey, for despite his to-ings and fro-ings from Chambers, there had been little opportunity of late to share a quiet hour alone with

Kate. Tomorrow, however, that would be put to rights he mused happily as he drifted off into a fitful sleep.

There was a chill in the morning air as Kate arose from her bed. Shivering involuntarily she reached for the crocheted shawl on a nearby chair and wrapping it quickly about her shoulders tiptoed across the bedroom floor to the casement window. The eve of her wedding day had arrived at last she reflected, staring thoughtfully at the light covering of snow on the meadow. Soon, all the effort of the past few weeks would come to fruition and in their wake a whole new future would begin. It was too late now to confess her fears to Edwin, though a week ago she was sorely tempted. But then he had arrived at the cottage, jubilant at having acquired the services of an architect and reputable builder. She had neither the heart to curtail his enthusiasm or strength of character to admit her impropriety.

Suddenly a cloud of despondency overwhelmed her and in an effort to disperse futile meanderings she dressed hurriedly in her work attire and set about her chores. Although the hour was early there was much to be done. Edwin would call upon her at ten o'clock, so with renewed vigour she stripped the covers from the large new bed Edwin had purchased and remade it with fresh linen. Then having ensured that the room was tidy and everything in place for their return from Paris, she made her way down the steep narrow staircase.

Despite Dora's kind offer to accommodate them both it was Edwin's wish that after the honeymoon he and Kate return to the privacy of Pembleton farm. A decision to be admired on his part, for the cottage lacked many of the amenities to which he was accustomed. Indeed, in all fairness, Kate saw fit to point out the disadvantages. Nonetheless, Edwin was determined to have his way, insisting that her presence would offset any inconvenience. And as he would only be spending weekends with her until his work load from chambers had been decided, the shortness of the period would cause little discomfort.

When Kate finally entered the kitchen to make a cup of tea, her path was blocked by the quantity of gifts they had received from the villagers at Saturday's party. They were generous folk she concluded as she reflected upon the occasion and Dora and Gerald had done them proud by providing sufficient quantities of food and drink for all. Tom Barratt, Albert's nephew, had accompanied the proceedings on his tuneful accordion as planned and so pleasant was the evening that when the dancing and jollities finally came to an end it was well past midnight. Making a mental note to thank Dora once more for so successful an enterprise, Kate began the task of carrying the presents up to the spare bedroom until a more permanent resting place could be found. The latter took longer than expected and despite rising early, by the time she had completed the rest of her chores, she found herself hurrying to change her clothing before Edwin's arrival.

Promptly at ten o'clock Edwin's vehicle appeared at the gate, closely followed by that of Reginald Hamilton. Temperatures had risen somewhat and the light covering of snow that had looked so picturesque earlier, had thawed into a muddy swamp of slush beyond the cobbled yard. Undeterred by the sight Edwin gave a cheerful grin as he alighted from his car and after insisting that the others remain in the comfort of their vehicle, extended his arm towards the approaching figure of Kate.

The moment he had settled her into the passenger seat he produced a tartan travel rug and proceeded to wrap it snugly over her lap. "You are warm enough Kate?" he queried softly. His concern was touching and Kate's deep, brown eyes melted gratefully in response. At that moment Albert, who had been hovering by the cowshed, came over to help with the baggage and after a hasty farewell the parties wend their way to London.

Throughout the journey the sky remained a nondescript grey and by the wayside trees lacking foliage, appeared dormant, inert. The state of the weather however, did little to dampen Edwin's spirits and as they travelled along, he chatted away good naturedly. "My father had a great affinity with the countryside," he recalled fondly. "Indeed, when I was a child, on a day such as this, he would take great delight in explaining that despite its desolate air, the woods were alive with goblins, planning their strategy for mischievous escapades in the spring."

Kate turned towards him with a smile of amusement. "Your father was something of a romantic?"

"Yes I suppose he was," Edwin confirmed thoughtfully. "A benevolent man also and a marvellous spinner of tales. My mother openly adored him. You would have liked him Kate." His grey eyes softened as he glanced fleetingly in her direction.

Kate nodded her head in assent. "How long since their passing Edwin?" she asked quietly.

"Three years. It was a boating accident. A routine Sunday afternoon's outing with friends. My parents were good swimmers but alas, the undercurrent was too strong."

By the tone of his voice Kate sensed the memory of that day was still a painful one. At once she regretted her curiosity and began to apologise.

"No need," Edwin interrupted benevolently, "at the onset there was much grief, but in hindsight, the bond between them was such they would have wished to have departed this world together. In life in death, so to speak." Suddenly his reflective mood changed. "Not, I think, a suitable topic for the eve of our wedding," he commented with a sheepish grin.

"No matter," Kate urged, "the sharing of such moments bring us closer to one another."

Edwin's gaze was fixed upon the road ahead but she sensed a certain relief in him. "And your father Kate, was he fond of the country also?"

Kate delved into her past for recollection of her father's pleasures, but alas, none came to the fore. "In truth Edwin I do not know," she answered with sombre resignation. "Though I was born in the County of Herefordshire, we moved to the suburbs of London when father, a member of the clergy, was offered a position in the area. A short time later, mother became ill and took to her bed. Father was a strict disciplinarian, not an easy man to comprehend. Indeed, I cannot on any occasion recall the sound of laughter in the house." How strange Kate pondered, that she should know so little of those who had played so prominent a role in her early years.

Edwin sensed a melancholy in her silent meanderings and moving his left hand from the steering wheel momentarily, gave hers a comforting squeeze. "Kate, dear Kate, our life together will be a happy one and there will be much laughter I promise you." The line of his jaw took on a determined air and his fervent reassurance strengthened Kate's hopes for the future.

A short interval for lunch delayed the parties somewhat and it was almost half past three in the afternoon when they reached their destination. By now daylight was fast fading and a cold, sharp wind that had heightened during the last hour promised a frosty night. In contrast to the dismal climate the glaring brightness of an illuminated sign above the entrance of the Royal was an agreeable sight. As Edwin escorted his companions into the warmth of the foyer Victoria complimented him upon his choice of premises for their stay.

Heartened by such praise Edwin concealed his own unease and in a confident manner approached the reception area. After a brief conversation with the Manager a bellboy was summoned and their luggage promptly removed to the appropriate rooms. Whereupon the ladies, having assured the menfolk they would meet them shortly in the sumptuous lounge for tea, made their way to the nearby powder room.

Upon their return, with numbers complete, the gathering commandeered a cluster of deep, comfortable chairs set amongst the potted palms. Without further ado conversation began in earnest with many topics under scrutiny. A leisurely tea followed and such was the atmosphere of conviviality that when the lyrical chimes of a nearby grandfather clock struck six o'clock, they echoed in unison as to how swiftly time had passed. Nonetheless, having decided to retire to their rooms at this time in order to rest before changing for dinner, the party disbanded.

At exactly half-past seven in the evening, Kate, accompanied by Dora and Victoria, emerged from the lift onto the richly carpeted opulence of the reception area. Edwin stood with his companions, patiently awaiting their arrival. Despite a throng of newcomers blocking their path, Victoria spotted her host at once. Indeed, he was an imposing figure in an immaculately tailored dinner suit and black bow tie and the crisp whiteness of his dress shirt accentuated his newly acquired outdoor complexion. At that moment he looked across the room and smiled to acknowledge their presence.

"My," Victoria tutted, nudging Kate's elbow playfully, "I had not realized until now what a dashing figure your future husband cuts. You'll make a handsome couple to be sure."

Kate's lips parted in a smile of amusement, nonetheless, she observed the figure of Edwin with renewed interest as he made his way towards them. Scanning in depth his neatly groomed, fair hair, wide forehead and strong angular features, she concluded that her companion had made no idle boast. Indeed, Edwin emerged from the crowd like a modern day Sir Galahad and having forsaken country tweeds for more formal attire, commanded an air of sophistication that was most attractive. Only when he fingered his white wing tipped collar and black bow tie in an awkward fashion did she sense intuitively that he would be far happier at the village hall in Hengleford than here in the splendid surrounds of the Royal. Her heart went out to him and touched by the effort he had undergone to make their brief stay here a special one, she squeezed his hand in a spontaneous manner before slipping her arm through his.

"You look outstanding Kate," he remarked in a voice barely more than a whisper.

Kate's eyes brimmed with affection. "And in this arena," she stated proudly, gesticulating to the crowded room, "you are a handsome gladiator."

His eyebrows arched with a look of surprise. "Is my discomfort so obvious?" he queried with alarm.

Kate shook her head. "To none other than myself," she remarked comfortingly, " but promise me Edwin that when we reach Paris we shall dine in establishments where you will feel more at ease."

A smile of relief spread across his face, "Thank you Kate."

"For?"

"Confirming what I have always known."

"And what is that pray?"

"That you have the makings of a most caring wife," he concluded with a whimsical grin.

Kate's cheeks flushed with colour and she retorted impishly, "Ah, but only if I am allowed sustenance at regular intervals. Oh Edwin, I am so hungry." She confessed weakly.

Conversation between their companions halted at the sound of their laughter.

"Amusing tales we share after dinner Edwin." Victoria scolded, tapping him lightly on the arm with her evening purse.

"Then we must dine at once or Kate will be too frail to participate," he quipped good-naturedly.

On entering the dining room the Maitre D' greeted them with a smile and an air of efficiency. After a brief glance at his book resting on the nearby rostrum he led them up the wide open staircase to one of the many tables set upon the balcony overlooking the dance floor. The room was vast with enormous windows framed by lavish drapes of royal blue. Chandeliers, suspended from an ornate ceiling, twinkled like clusters of stars and below them to the left, a discreetly raised platform housed a small orchestra.

"What a magnificent view we have of the proceedings," Victoria enthused as she placed her purse on the balcony rail beside her. "Edwin my dear, you are a jewel. If I was unmarried and thirty years younger I would seek your attentions myself," she jested.

"And I would find it difficult to ignore such advances," Edwin retaliated gallantly.

A hail of laughter from the rest of the party set the mood of the evening and it remained so until its conclusion.

Normal routine is not easily discarded and when Kate awoke at five o'clock in the morning she found it most pleasurable to linger beneath the covers of the large, comfortable bed and contemplate leisurely upon the day's events. Her itinerary ran thus:

9am Breakfast.

10.15 am The hired limousine takes the wedding party to the registrar's office.

10.45 am Wedding ceremony.

12 noon. Return to the Royal as Mrs Edwin Jameson and play hostess at a celebratory lunch for her dear friends.

The day would continue to be a full one until she and Edwin departed for the boat train in the evening. Had it not been for niggling doubts as to her physical condition, she could have committed herself to the proceedings with vigorous enthusiasm. As it was, her mood oscillated between moments of anxiety to unexpected bouts of buoyancy, which in the face of all Edwin's efforts seemed totally ungrateful on her part. Perhaps the trauma of the last few weeks had delayed her menstrual cycle she ruminated hopefully. There was still no sign of it and yet her body functioned well without hint of anything untoward. In truth she sighed, she must close her mind to such misgivings and intensify her energies into making her marriage a happy one.

Suddenly, in an all-embracing effort to rid herself of mindless wavering she rose from her bed stretched her arms luxuriously into the air and set about preparing her wardrobe for the day's engagements.

Much to Edwin's relief, by half past one in the afternoon, arrangements had passed without the merest hint of a dilemma. And whilst he complimented himself for a portion of its success, the majority of it was to his mind attributed to the presence of such jovial companions. They were, he mused, eyeing the group fondly as they seated themselves at the dining table, a benevolent party, committed wholeheartedly to the happy occasion. Indeed, throughout the wedding ceremony he had been grateful for their support and now, as the sound of their social intercourse accompanied the feasting, he experienced a feeling of complete euphoria in their presence.

Instinctively his gaze wandered the length of the table to Kate, bedecked in an ivory coloured satin costume with an orchid attached to the lapel of her jacket. It was a tasteful outfit he thought, befitting exactly the requirements of a registry office. And for an accessory the choker of pearls at the base of her neck was not overly done. Merely a subtle indication as to the slender line of her throat. He pondered once more upon his good fortune and as he viewed the gentle curve of her bosom his body ached with longing. When he looked up Kate's deep, brown eyes penetrated his own and his face coloured with embarrassment. He felt like a schoolboy caught in the act of some mischievous deed. Yet she smiled openly with a tantalizing look of innocence and there was no hint of reprimand in the soft eiderdown of her gaze. Their eyes held until Victoria leaned towards Kate and murmured something in her ear, at which point Gerald Parkins, encouraged by the rest of the party, rose to his feet.

"I must confess," Gerald exclaimed with a smile, "speeches are not my forte. However, on this occasion it is only fitting that I attempt to voice what is in my heart." He paused, clearing his throat noisily before continuing. "Both Dora and I look upon Katherine as if she were our own and as such our concern is for her happiness and wellbeing. That you dear boy," he remarked, shifting his gaze to Edwin, "so obviously share the same view, is of special comfort to us. Therefore may you both harvest the fruits of your love, find comfort always in each other and in future years look back upon this day with fond and loving recall. Dear friends, I ask you to raise your glasses and toast the happy couple."

"Katherine and Edwin," his companions echoed before sipping their champagne.

Shortly after seven o'clock Kate disappeared briefly to change into her lengthy, tweed travelling skirt. It was complemented perfectly by a light, chocolate coloured woollen and smart, leather ankle boots upon her feet. After packing the last of her wedding attire into the suitcase she closed it in preparation for the hotel porter who was due to despatch it shortly. Looking into the mirror she put the final touches to her hair and lifting the new camel coloured coat from the coat hook behind the door, made her way downstairs.

It was almost eight o'clock when the bride and groom took their leave. Bidding their companions farewell they left the warmth of the Royal and stepped with their luggage into the cold night air towards the waiting car. As luck would have it, the night express from Victoria station departed promptly at a quarter to nine and by half past ten, the locomotive had reached the departure point at Newhaven harbour. Formalities at the passenger terminal were quickly over and soon the newlyweds alighted the gangway where a waiting steward showed them to their cabin.

The sleeping quarters were adequate with luxurious fittings. A bottle of champagne rested in an ice bucket on the dresser, a kind gesture on behalf of the shipping company. Satisfied that the accommodation was to their liking, Edwin deposited a generous tip in the steward's hand and after a respectful goodnight, the young man left, closing the door behind him.

"Well my dear," Edwin stated, removing a timepiece from his waistcoat pocket and eyeing it thoughtfully, "we shall be sailing soon. Would you care to take a short stroll around the deck before retiring, or are you too weary after such an exhausting day?"

In truth, the day had been a demanding one and had prompted a heady restlessness. She welcomed the opportunity to walk awhile. She smiled agreeably as she removed the warm worsted coat from her shoulder. "The fresh air will clear my thoughts a little," she replied. "Give me a moment or two to unpack my overnight bag Edwin and I shall be pleased to accompany you."

When eventually they left the cabin and ascended the narrow stairwell the sanctuary of the harbour had long since departed. An abundance of stars dotted the velvet night sky and the moon, full and round, reflected a channel of light upon the sea as the ship ploughed its way in a cumbersome fashion through the deep, dark waters. Kate clutched the handrail of the upper deck to steady her body against a sudden buffeting wind and caught her breath as the force of it gathered momentum.

At once Edwin was behind her, his muscular frame shielding her back. "Are you all right Kate?" he shouted, folding his arms about her for protection.

The ship dipped low then rose like a whale out of the water. Prompted by a feeling of exhilaration she nodded her head excitedly. It was as if the elements had gathered in unison to perform this mighty extravaganza; as the front of her coat billowed in the relentless breeze, the spray of the sea cleansed her features and her mind was purged of doubt.

Edwin leaned over her shoulder. "Happy?" He queried affectionately in her ear.

Relief and elation flooded Kate's being as she turned in his embrace to face him. "I am overjoyed Edwin. Truly," she exclaimed above the noise of the whining wind.

Suddenly the light of the moon illuminated her features. As Edwin stared at this wondrous creature with fire in her eyes and hair strewn across her face in such a wild abandoned fashion his passion soared. Eagerly he pressed his lips against the coolness of her cheek. "If ever a bride looked lovelier I have yet to know of it," he murmured reverently. "But come my dear, we must return to the cabin before you take a chill."

CHAPTER EIGHT

On their return from Paris, Kate and Edwin set about their life together with the months that followed proving a period of great joy. Not that it was an entirely satisfactory arrangement, with Edwin busy at his chambers for much of the week. But both individuals thrived upon hard work and Kate accepted his temporary absences with good heart. She knew he planned to spend more time at home once they were settled in their own premises at Longlea Meadow, the name they had decided upon for the house that they were to build together.

Despite brief reunions, they found time to discuss plans for the future which included on one occasion, Kate's eagerness to purchase the land adjacent to Pembleton farm. The latter belonged to sheep farmer Josiah Tebbutt, an ailing seventy-five year old, who lacked the physical strength to continue. The matter was of some urgency as the fellow had no son and heir to inspire him to carry on and he wanted to rid himself of all responsibility before the beginnings of another winter. Edwin could see the logic of such an acquisition and as Kate seemed intent on purchasing the land plus a modest flock of sheep to whit, he assisted with much of the negotiating and legal work on her behalf.

Meanwhile, plans for the house were constantly being revised. Although the bleak winter had delayed its start, by early spring the footings had been prepared and building had begun in earnest. A certain amount of effort on the contractor's part and the promise of a monetary bonus from Edwin ensured that, but for minor details, all would be complete by the end of May. Kate had followed its progress with constant regularity but only when Edwin ceremoniously handed her the keys and they stepped over the threshold of the property did she realise the true dimensions of it. Gone at last were the tools, ladders and paraphernalia belonging to the workmen. All that remained were large, bare expanses of space. Suddenly the prospect of transforming the property into a comfortable habitat seemed a daunting one.

Nonetheless, as she moved from room to room Kate began to visualise suitable items she had seen in a catalogue Edwin had brought from London. On ascending the wide, sweeping staircase, excitement mounted for the task of furnishing their first real home together. Edwin followed her as she walked over to the large, sash windows of their bedroom and when he reached her side, he placed his arm affectionately about her shoulders. Together, in silence, they gazed out at the picturesque landscape surrounding Pembleton farm.

A sudden warm spell had encouraged the flowering of the six-foot high hawthorn hedges interspersed with ash and elm trees. And on this bright, spring-like day, the neat division of green fields and buttercup dotted meadows, was a view to be envied. Indeed, the tranquillity and peacefulness of it all encouraged Kate's thoughts to run amok and as she considered the preparatory work ahead of her she swivelled in her husband's embrace.

"Furniture Edwin," she gasped. "So much is needed. How on earth are we going to provide the house with sufficient quantities of it?"

"You my dear," he smiled teasingly, "must journey up to London on Friday morning and we shall go together to the showroom to choose what is necessary and confirm the items you have already chosen from the catalogue. No excuses now. I will have someone meet you at St. Pancras and bring you back to chambers. You have yet to see chambers, or for that matter my living quarters. Are you not curious?"

"I am of course," she began in a perturbed fashion, "but Friday is…"

"I know," he interrupted, "market day. Young Ted was hoping that you had sufficient confidence in him to carry off the particular task of looking after the property whilst Albert and Archie went to market as usual."

"Oh?" she queried, her forehead puckering attractively into an enquiring frown.

"I have already arranged the matter with Albert, not that I would be so presumptuous as to interfere in the normal course of events, but I have engaged a room for us at the Royal for the weekend. It was to be something of a surprise."

The statement was matter of fact, to the point, but Kate's face glowed with pleasure as she pecked him affectionately upon his cheek. "I am so fortunate to be your wife," she concluded happily.

Edwin studied her features lovingly, his fingers gently smoothing a fallen lock of hair from her forehead. He felt humbled by this beautiful, capable, childlike creature who gave herself to him so utterly and completely. In truth, any deed he could perform to perpetuate her happiness was to good effect. "I agree," he remarked playfully, for fear of displaying his vulnerability.

Tut tutting at such immodesty Kate released herself from his arms and continued to survey the rest of the house. Happily, Edwin followed in her footsteps. "By the way, should you arrive in good time on Friday, there is a strong possibility you will meet brother Charles. His absences are far less frequent from chambers since marriage to Annabel."

"Her influence you think?" Kate remarked lightly over her shoulder.

"Possibly," he pondered. "However, to more important matters. I have here at my disposal one measure, notebook and pencil. I suggest we begin with requirements for each room."

If Kate was apprehensive at the mention of his brother she did not show it. But in the early hours of Monday morning when Edwin had departed for London , she allowed her thoughts to ramble. She had no desire to meet with Charles now or ever, but for obvious reasons it would be impossible to avoid him indefinitely. Nonetheless, there was no spark of enthusiasm on her part. Such feelings for him had long since departed. Indeed, over the past few months she had regained her confidence. And having borne a light menstrual period, the first since her marriage, she no longer had doubts as to the tragic affair that had caused so much heartache. Her physical condition had never been better she mused. Aside from putting on a little weight, which she attributed to a life of flourishing contentment, the unfortunate incident with Charles was thankfully behind her.

When Friday morning came and Albert drove her to the station in the pony and trap, her confidence began to wane a little. However, the journey was pleasant enough and on arrival at St. Pancras she was about to step out of the railway carriage when a voice called, "There you are." A moment later Charles was at her side assisting her on to the platform. "I overheard our efficient Miss Bartholomew arranging for someone to meet you. How fortunate I had no further appointments until after two," he grinned. His deep, blue eyes scanned her features approvingly. "My dear, marriage to that brother of mine suits you well," he remarked lightly, his lips brushing her cheek in an affectionate manner.

"Thank you, Charles," she acknowledged with a smile, looking at him directly as she buttoned the warm, worsted cape about her shoulders. He had lost none of his fine-looking features she mused. A few grey hairs mingled with the rest perhaps, but they merely accentuated his distinguished air. Once again the memory of her past foolishness was a source of embarrassment. For to think that the last time they met he had proposed marriage and she had accepted. How cruel the games he played with little thought for the hurt caused.

"As it is almost eleven o'clock, I suggest we take a short break for refreshments before moving on to chambers," he stated confidently, taking her arm and leading her towards the exit.

"I think not," Kate replied firmly. "Edwin is expecting me and we have much to do before close of day." The tone of her voice implied that there was little chance of persuading her otherwise.

"As you wish," he remarked grudgingly, smarting a little from the rebuff.

They walked in silence toward the waiting taxi and when Kate was seated he moved in beside her. A moment later the engine spluttered to life and as they travelled through the busy streets of London Charles attempted once more to weaken her resolve. "I would have liked the opportunity to speak with you alone," he murmured in an intimate fashion.

Kate turned in her seat to study the features of the handsome, spoilt individual that had once seemed so appealing. "Why?" she asked in a forthright manner.

The request was a simple one but it prompted confrontation. Taken aback by her bluntness Charles lost sight of the plea he had so carefully rehearsed that morning. His silence induced a marked victory for Kate and inspired by such an advantage she took the matter into her own hands.

"Perhaps you wish to clear your conscience?" she continued quietly. "No need. But to quell any misunderstanding that may occur in the future, I have to speak my mind. Both you and I are aware that you had no intention ever of taking our relationship any further than it is today. I was foolish to have believed otherwise. Since that unfortunate incident however, we have both committed ourselves in marriage to other partners. I for one consider myself blessed. You too no doubt. Therefore, would it not be more favourable to consider a pact of polite aloofness. I hold no lasting grudge and all you will have suffered is a slight denting of the ego," she concluded.

Charles was stunned by her words and a moment passed before he regained his composure. Then suddenly a mischievous grin broke out upon his face and he gave a hearty laugh. "Bravo," he applauded, clapping his hands together with enthusiasm. "Katherine, I adore you. Were others of your gender so candid. As to your pact I am willing, with certain reservations as to the degree of aloofness required. Here's my hand on it."

Kate stretched out her hand and he shook it vigorously. Was that a look of relief upon his face? Had she been as much of a threat to Charles as he had appeared to her?

It was a glorious June, colourful, delightfully picturesque and undeniably hot. For much of the month the sun had shone from an azure blue sky, expelling a heat sufficient to sap the strength of the most ardent sun worshipper.

Throughout this period Kate toiled unstintingly to prepare the marital home. Although at times feeling decidedly out of sorts she attributed her condition to the extra work that had evolved from the acquisition of Josiah Tebbutt's land. Under Albert's watchful eye plans were well afoot to attempt a period of sheep farming and two experienced hands from the tiny hamlet of nearby Washbrook had been set on to assist in the venture.

About this time young Ted showed himself to be a most reliable asset. After much deliberation it was Kate's wish that, after she and Edwin moved into Longlea meadow, she would establish him in the cottage at Pembleton farm if he so wished. Having installed running water and electricity at Longlea it seemed appropriate also that with extra funding the cottage too should be renovated and brought up to the high standards deserving of the year 1913. This was after all, a new, exciting era.

Ted accepted her proposal eagerly. Indeed, it was an offer to be envied by many of his contemporaries, for work was scarce and the prospect of housing more so.

So the young man's future was set and Emily the local girl he had been courting could begin to make plans for their life together. It was satisfying to assist in the happiness of another Kate mused philosophically as she listened to Ted's earnest intentions. A moment later Albert appeared at the barn door. Knowing the purpose of their discussion he began to rib the youth in a jovial manner with regard to wives and their ilk.

By the month of July Longlea Meadow was ready for occupation. The time could not have been more opportune as the coming Saturday was Edwin's birthday. By way of celebration, Edwin had persuaded Kate to journey to London on the Friday although had he been aware that the house would be habitable so soon, he would no doubt have cancelled the trip. However, arrangements had been made. As the weekend would commence with a stay at the Royal and later include seats to a concert at the Albert Hall, Kate had no wish to telephone him the news and disrupt his plans. The concert was to precede Edwin's much needed two week rest from chambers and as it added a somewhat celebratory flavour to the proceedings, the readiness of their new home would lose nothing by awaiting their return on Sunday. Kate's accomplishments with regard to the property could only prolong his good spirits. And so it was that with a happy heart on this bright July morning, Kate alighted the train and began her journey to London.

Mr Peabody, Edwin's clerk, met her on arrival at St. Pancras station. A slight, balding little man, he made himself known to her and with well-mannered efficiency escorted her to the waiting taxi. It was at this point that Kate experienced a severe pain in her abdomen, causing her to double over in agony and collapse onto her seat. At once the cabbie suggested he drive them straight to the nearest hospital. Mr Peabody was flummoxed to say the least. After all, his morning had begun with the simple task of escorting his employer's wife back to chambers, yet, here he was, in a situation completely foreign to a bachelor of his years. Nonetheless, he did his best to comfort Kate in her distress. On reaching the casualty department of the hospital he was relieved to deposit her into the hands of those more capable in dealing with such matters. His pale, strained features prompted one of the nurses to bring him a chair. Once he had sat upon it a moment and gathered his senses, he assured her that he would notify his employer of the dilemma the minute he returned to his place of work. Whereupon, a cup of sweet tea was offered, which he took gratefully into his trembling hands. After a short interval, having answered the only question he could with regard to Kate's next of kin, he made a hasty exit back to chambers.

By now Kate's discomfort had worsened and as the nurse at her side relieved her of her clothing a young doctor emerged from behind a loose screen. "Mrs. Jameson," he stated calmly, glancing quickly at the notes in his hand, "I am going to examine you, so try to relax a little." Placing her notes on the top of a nearby cabinet he proceeded to examine her stomach gently with his hands.

Kate attempted to speak but suddenly the pain worsened and she felt nauseous.

The doctor turned at once to the member of staff at his side. "Prepare the labour room immediately."

At exactly three o'clock in the afternoon, Kate gave birth to a son weighing almost six and a half pounds. Shocked and weakened by the trauma of the unexpected event she was placed in a side ward of the hospital where with curtains drawn she slumbered peacefully until the pale light of dawn. When she finally opened her eyes, in a blurred, somewhat hazy fashion, she saw the figure of Edwin standing by the open curtain of the window. Sensing her awareness between the crisp, white bed-sheets he turned instinctively and moved towards her. Tears of relief welled in his grey eyes and as he sat upon the chair at her bedside, he cupped his hands protectively over hers. "Kate, my dearest Kate, we have a son," he murmured, leaning over to place a kiss upon her damp forehead.

Her throat felt dry and painful and a look of consternation crossed her pale features as she scanned the room for sign of him. "Is he well?" she questioned weakly.

"Indeed yes," he enthused quietly. "A slight breathing difficulty, but it is not unusual I understand."

Kate winced as she attempted to change her position in the bed.

"Are you in great pain my darling?" Edwin asked anxiously as he observed the beads of perspiration upon her brow.

She shook her head drowsily. "A little weary that is all, my dear." She sighed, finding it difficult to keep her eyelids from closing.

"Then you must rest dearest," he insisted softly. "Sleep now, I shall stay with you a while longer."

For Edwin, the next few days became fraught with anxiety. Kate was smitten with an infection that sent her temperature soaring and for hours she lay in the starkness of the hospital cot rolling from side to side in a state of delirium. Several days passed before her condition had stabilized and it wasn't until her pulse and colour returned to normal, that she began to pine for a glimpse of her baby son.

Noting the overall improvement of her physical condition, the doctor at last declared her well enough to be accompanied in a wheel chair to the hospital nursery, though for the present, she was only permitted to view the little one through the narrow paned glass window. When Kate finally caught sight of the tiny bundle with black hair, fragile limbs and excessively yellow skin, her fears for him grew and in her weakened state she fretted openly. Coolly, but confidently, those in charge of his well-being dismissed her melancholy and assured her that despite having made such a dramatic entrance into the world, his progress was excellent. Whereupon Kate departed, having no reason to doubt their adamant reassurances.

Meanwhile, Edwin busied himself at chambers, having concluded that it would be more beneficial to take a holiday when Kate and the little fellow were discharged from hospital. Since Kate's steady progress, his appearances at the hospital had been somewhat curtailed by the rigid regulations concerning visiting hours. In truth, on one occasion, through no fault of his own, he had arrived too late to be admitted and when he voiced his dismay to the receptionist, she informed him in no uncertain terms that the rules were set to benefit the welfare of the patient, not, she said tersely, for the convenience of visitors. It was an experience he did not care to repeat and after depositing a large box of chocolates in her care, left the premises somewhat dejected by the reprimand.

The following evening, he had sat at his wife's bedside and with a woebegone expression spoke of the scathing lecture he had received. As a patient, Kate was fully aware of the abrasive manner of some in charge and she had smiled with amusement at the image of a deposed Edwin, brought about by a slip of a girl to boot. Indeed, the description of it first-hand had encouraged a ripple of laughter, an action that allayed any doubts Edwin may have had as to her recovery. Nonetheless, the matter prompted him to ask if she would care to be transferred to a nursing home more befitting their circumstances. At once Kate declined. After all, there was little point in such an upheaval, as she and the little one were both progressing well and in a short time they would all be together at Longlea meadow.

Cheered by such optimism, Edwin scanned her features affectionately. A renewed vigour shone in her deep, brown eyes as she spoke of the tasks in hand and her delicate cheeks bore a good colour from the enforced rest. There were moments of late he had thought he would lose her and, when he was alone, the vivid memory of those times would send a shiver of terror down his spine. Although it was a brief, fleeting experience, he would not care to endure such a period again.

"There will be much to do upon my return," Kate remarked eagerly, dispersing his thoughts.

"Ah, that reminds me," Edwin stated efficiently, "I have heard from Dora. She and Gerald have prepared a room at Longlea in readiness for the little fellow with all the items you have listed."

Kate's eyes sparkled at the prospect of viewing the nursery. "Before all else Edwin you must decide upon a name for our son," she implored. "We cannot forever refer to him as the little fellow."

"In truth, I was of the mind that you might wish to…" With a nod in her direction he left his sentence unfinished.

"What was your father's first name?" she queried patiently.

"Edward."

"Then we shall call him Edward Albert Jameson," Kate stated proudly.

Edwin beamed with pleasure and leaning forward placed a kiss upon her forehead. "You are becoming something of a genius Mrs Jameson," he commented teasingly.

"For modesty's sake I shall refrain from agreeing," she replied demurely.

"Oh, and before it slips my memory completely, Albert and Ted have done wonders with the cottage in your absence and both send..." He broke off at the sound of the bell requesting visitors to depart, "their best wishes for a hasty recovery. Now I must be off," he concluded, feigning a look of alarm as he rose to his feet. "Before I receive another scolding."

Kate laughed outright at his pretence of discomfort, but affection showed in her eyes as she observed his departure. How fortunate she was and how exciting the future would be she mused happily.

Her continued improvement resulted in a move from the tranquillity of the side room into the long narrow eight -bedded maternity ward that was all too often bustling with various activities. As Kate was only too aware, babies had no notion of timing. From the early hours of the morning until late into the night, there were disturbances of one kind or another. Pleased as she was to have the companionship of others, there were times she found it impossible to get to sleep and on one such occasion had to call upon Grace, the night duty nurse, for something to assist her slumber.

With fair, short-cropped hair, pretty features and startling green eyes, Grace was a senior nurse in her early thirties. Out of all the staff on the labour ward she was the patients' favourite. She was cheerful and efficient, yet had an approachable air, which was something the doctors lacked. Indeed, should anyone be so bold as to voice a query to the doctor, they received a look implying impertinence. And that prompted a certain unease, whereupon the recipient was overcome by a feeling of inadequacy and mortification. Perhaps such vulnerability arose from being both physically and mentally exposed.

That very evening, after Edwin's departure, the ward was unusually quiet and everyone but Kate fast asleep. Grace noted her restlessness and having finished the paperwork upon her desk approached Kate's bed. Drawing up a chair she sat beside her and said, "If all goes well, you should be returning home at the end of the week."

Kate looked startled and resting on her elbows edged her way up the mattress until her back was leaning against the pillows for support. "And baby Edward?"

"So," Grace acknowledged with a smile," you have named him officially at last. Yes, tomorrow we shall be showing you how to bathe him and give general advice as to his welfare."

Kate's excitement for the morning was suddenly tinged with trepidation. It was an overwhelming thought, holding little Edward for more than a moment as she had done over the last few days. Even the latter had taken place under the watchful eyes of hospital staff and there was great comfort to be had by their presence.

"Come now," Grace assured her, "It's really not so terrifying. You'll see."

"Grace, tell me," a look of consternation clouded Kate's features ,"how could I not have known all these months that I was carrying a child?"

"On occasion it happens," her mentor replied thoughtfully. "The usual symptoms do not show themselves. Sometimes there is a slight bleeding which women interpret as a sign of menstruation. There are many reasons, all of which would baffle you further to be truthful."

"But little Edward was premature," she replied quickly.

Grace rose from her chair and walked over to her desk. Then taking the relevant papers from her files she returned to Kate's bed. "Only a day or two I would suspect. Nothing of great significance," she replied, still scanning the notes in her hand.

"But he is in the nursery for premature babies," Kate insisted, grasping at the last thread of hope.

"It was necessary because he had made such a hasty entry into the world. And at that time the poor little mite was jaundiced, underweight and in shock; no, rest assured he was not premature in the true sense of the word."

"Then I must have conceived..." Kate broke off to mentally accumulate the months.

"According to my calculations you must have conceived the child late September or early October," Grace stated confidently. "Now my dear, the hour is late and you need your rest. Take this mild sedative," she ordered kindly, passing Kate a drink of water and smoothing the sheets on her bed. "Goodnight Mrs Jameson."

"Goodnight Grace," Kate reiterated, sliding her body between the sheets and staring woefully up at the ceiling. In truth, before this, she had not suspected anything untoward concerning the birth of little Edward. Edwin too must have accepted without question the premature notice above the nursery door. Then later, having been mesmerized by her condition, would have been so overwhelmed by events as to not inquire further. It would appear that most gentlemen were unaccustomed to delving into matters of a private nature, so it would be left to Kate to query any details relevant to the birth. Suddenly her blood ran cold. Should Edwin discover the same knowledge as she was a thought too distressing to contemplate.

Her reluctance to confess all to Edwin at the beginning of their relationship had prompted one apprehension after another. She could see that now. Yet how confident she had been in November when a slight period had appeared. It was as if she had been given a second chance and at that point partly to appease her conscience, she had thrown herself wholeheartedly into the task of making Edwin a good wife. Nonetheless, as the months passed by, her affection for this gentle, sensitive man gradually blossomed into love. And since that time their union had been blessed with a total confidence in one another. Dare she now divulge the news of her impropriety and jeopardize all that had gone before? Was his love for her strong enough to withstand such a blow?

Dear God, were that she could turn back the clock and begin life anew from the very moment of Edwin's arrival. In truth, such deceit could not go on she pondered ruefully. It would eat away at the very foundation of their life together. No, she had shied away from the responsibility far too long. When the time was right she would voice the burden and throw herself upon his mercy.

During the first week of August Kate was discharged from the hospital. It was with mixed feelings that she bade farewell to the nursing staff and set off with Edwin and little Edward for the return journey to Longlea meadow. As they travelled the winding lanes homeward, she stared out of the car window, silent and uncommunicative. Her stay of almost four weeks in the side and maternity wards at the hospital had, on occasion, a smothering effect. But it was a secure place, one that bore little relation to the outside world. Now, in the vastness of the open countryside, she felt confused and strangely disorientated. Indeed, half-heartedly, she wished she were back taking part in the rigid but custodial routine of the hospital. Nonsense, her conscience chided, which it was of course. For at heart she was longing to return home with little Edward and for that matter to witness Edwin's pleasure when he took note of her accomplishments with regard to the house.

In an effort to resume with some kind of normality, she checked the milk bottles in the small bag that the nurse had provided and pulled a light cover over little Edward who was sleeping peacefully on the back seat beside her. The infant looked almost cherubic, swathed in a cream flannelette nightgown and set amongst the well-packed blankets that provided his makeshift bed. As she touched his cheek with her hand to assure herself that he was sufficiently warm, she was moved by such a depth of feeling towards him that tears glistened in her deep, brown eyes. That this tiny creature relied solely upon her for his well-being was an awe inspiring task and one that must be taken into account before confessing all to Edwin.

Throughout the journey Edwin did not press her to discuss or communicate her thoughts in any way, as he was fully aware of the strain she had undergone. And so, from time to time, he would merely mention snippets of news that sprang to mind. Despite the bright sunlight there was a cool breeze and for this reason when he asked if Kate wished to stop, so she might stretch her legs a little, she concluded it would be best to move on without delay. Eventually they reached the outlying meadows of Pembleton farm and with relief Kate caught a glimpse of their house Longlea meadow.

"Almost there," Edwin commented with a smile "How is little Edward?"

"Well," she assured him softly as they approached the entrance and the car turned slowly into the driveway.

Dora and Gerald Parkins greeted them eagerly on their arrival. Having had access to the property they had taken the liberty of preparing a light tea in readiness in the sitting room. "Ours is but a short stay, my dear," Dora exclaimed, pecking Kate on the cheek and relieving her of the infant whilst Kate removed her light coat.

"Truth now, Dora," Gerald laughed, shaking Edwin by the hand. "You wanted to be the first to see little Edward here, did you not?"

Dora's eyes lit up and her full cheeks blossomed with a smug smile as she nursed the little one close to her chest. "Take no notice, for Gerald has been just as anxious. Now sit yourselves down and sample the sandwiches, do. In the kitchen there is a steak pie I have baked in preparation for your supper this evening, so this is merely a light tea to sustain you until then."

"I must say the food looks most appetising, Dora," Edwin commented, reaching for a plate.

"Indeed yes," Kate seconded gratefully as she helped herself to a sandwich.

Dora preened. "I put a match to the fire in here as the room felt a little chilly." She continued informatively. " Your bed is well aired, the larder is well stocked, oh and Ted's mother is popping in tomorrow morning as you suggested Edwin, to see how she can best assist you."

"Oh?" Kate's eyebrows arched with curiosity as she looked at her husband.

"Thank you Dora," Edwin replied, shifting his gaze toward Kate. " I had thought that with all the farm business to organize and little Edward here, you would be needing someone to help with the house work. In the nature of a part time housekeeper, or just as you see fit," he concluded, hoping to convince her of his good intentions.

Kate's eyes shone with gratitude, "That was most thoughtful of you Edwin. I am sure Mrs Porter and I can come to some satisfactory arrangement."

Standing with his back to the fire, Gerald Parkins sipped his tea and looked perceptively around the room. "You have done wonders with this place in so short a time Katherine," he stated admiringly.

"Edwin has yet to make a tour of the premises," she laughed. "Indeed I do believe his birthday present is still untouched in the study."

Edwin gave a feigned look of surprise. "I had thought little Edward was my birthday gift," he stated whimsically. "In that case I shall look forward to the discovery later."

The clock on the mantelpiece chimed six o'clock and Gerald cast an anxious look at Dora. "Come my dear, we must away and leave the young ones to settle in."

"Of course," Dora agreed, "shall I help you with the dishes before we go my dear?"

"No, please," Kate insisted, relieving Dora of the plates already in her hand. "You have done so much already, what with the preparation of the nursery and so much more."

"Ah, now, when you go upstairs," Dora continued quickly, "I'm sure you will have no difficulty in finding the items that you need. The drawers are placed such that little Edward's undergarments are in the bottom one and upwards to his top clothes."

Kate smiled in admiration. "You are a treasure. What would we have done without your assistance."

"Oh, 'tis nothing child." Dora's cheeks flushed with colour as she dismissed the compliment. "Now Gerald, we must tarry no longer."

Gerald's face bore a look of forbearance, "Did I not say the very same thing but half an hour ago?" he remarked jokingly as he moved towards the door.

"Let me escort you to the car," Edwin remarked as he helped Dora into her coat. "No doubt I shall be driving into the village sometime over the next few days. I'll make a point of calling in on you."

In the stillness after her guests had departed, Kate wandered over to the couch and picked up little Edward who had begun to whimper. The infant stirred and yet, as she cradled him in her arms he yawned, sighed and drifted off into another sleep. "Come, little one," she murmured against the softness of his cheek. "To the nursery we go. You will be more comfortable there."

With Edward safely cradled in the crook of her left arm, she lifted the small bag containing his bottle and essentials with her free hand and carefully mounted the wide staircase. The door of the bedroom adjacent to the master was wide open and as Kate stepped inside, the full extent of her dear friends' efforts took her breath away. There was a fire burning in the grate, a bucket filled with small coals beside it and a brass guard in front for safety's sake. For this Kate was especially grateful, as the house might have appeared somewhat chilly to Edward, having come from the warm temperatures of the hospital.

Not only that, but all the items Edwin had ordered from the furniture store had been delivered and placed in perfect positions about the room even to the nursing chair and crib. The changing table was already prepared with towel and napkins and as she turned her eyes caught sight of a splendid rocking horse set in the corner. It was, she discovered on looking at the card attached to its saddle, a gift from Dora and Gerald. Their generosity was boundless she mused.

Little Edward rallied sufficient to take his bottle feed and after she had changed his napkin, she placed him gently down into the comfort of the freshly made crib. At that moment Edwin entered the nursery and put his arm affectionately about her shoulders. "We are blessed with good friends are we not?" he said, unquestionably moved by their support and ready willingness to be of assistance.

Kate turned in his embrace and leaned her head against his chest. "We are indeed. So much so that I wonder if I might suggest…" with the sentence unfinished she raised her head.

Edwin looked down into her deep, brown eyes. "Yes my dear, what is it?"

"Could we add Gerald's name to follow Edward Albert on the registration form?"

He lowered his head and kissed her gently on the lips. "I think that to be a splendid proposal. I shall arrange it on my return to London."

CHAPTER NINE

No sooner than Kate had settled into Longlea Meadow than matters concerning the farm which only she and Albert could resolve, needed urgent attention. Inevitably one task led to another and before long, despite the aid of Mrs Porter, her days became fully occupied. Nonetheless it was a rewarding time. Whenever Edwin was at home, he spent many hours leaning over the cot in the nursery just gazing at little Edward, or entertaining him in his arms when he was awake. The bonding was a joy to observe.

As weeks slipped quickly into months, Kate had yet to find an appropriate moment to broach the subject with Edwin. In truth, as time distanced itself, she questioned the relevance of such a disclosure. The likelihood of the matter ever coming to light was dubious to say the least. Although she had to admit on the odd occasion Edwin provided news of his brother, fears for the eventual outcome of it all weighed heavy on her conscience. Indeed, when he spoke of being approached by Annabel to discuss Charles's involvement with another woman, all the guilt she had so cleverly concealed rushed to the fore. Poor Edwin she pondered ruefully. He suffered from all sides. First with Annabel's unannounced visitation at chambers, then during working hours with Charles, who insisted that his wife was behaving like a spoilt child.

The unburdening of their marital problems however, only saw fit to confirm to Edwin how lucky he was and that evening he had said as much to Kate. Dear God, after such a statement, how could she destroy a way of life that had become so precious to them both? Apart from disturbing moments such as the latter, each day had settled into a pleasurable routine of activity, with Edwin content to work at chambers from Monday to Thursday lunchtime and returning to Hengleford for the duration of the week. Much of his leisure time was still occupied by little Edward, who by now was progressing into a bonny, contented boy. That Edwin doted upon the child was a fact Kate found truly encouraging.

Christmas came and went with all the special delights that go into the making of the season. Nonetheless, it was a particularly long, hard winter, with insurmountable snow drifts that on occasion prevented Edwin from returning to London. By the middle of March however, whilst few crocus' remained, in the nearby copse bluebells appeared to herald the arrival of spring. Indeed, everything was alive and growing, just waiting in readiness for the warmth of the sun before blossoming into a blaze of colour.

Influenced by this sense of new beginnings was Kate's decision to reveal to Edwin this very weekend upon the matter that she had kept from him far too long. During the last few months she had appeased her conscience with one excuse after another, but now, however painful the consequences, she would face up to the task or put it behind her forever. There would be no more dilly dallying. Once again however, unforeseen events were set to delay Kate's revelation. For when Edwin arrived home at supper time on Thursday evening, hours later than was usual, he brought with him disturbing news.

"Brother Charles has plans to relinquish our partnership," he announced as he unbuttoned his sombre suit jacket and seated himself wearily upon the couch in the sitting room.

Kate caught her breath with surprise as she filled his glass with sherry from the decanter. "Leave the practice?" she queried, trembling slightly as she moved forward and placed his drink upon the table at his side.

"Yes," Edwin replied flatly. "He wishes to dissolve our partnership and take up a position offered by Annabel's father."

"But why, Edwin? What has brought about such a decision?" Kate asked, seating herself beside him.

"Earlier in the week Annabel created another scene at chambers with regard to Charles's infidelity," he began.

"Go on," Kate urged her features taut and flushed with colour.

"There has been talk in the city over the last few weeks, but," Edwin gesticulated with his hands in exasperation, "the man's a fool, a complete and utter fool."

Numbed by his news, Kate waited patiently until Edwin saw fit to continue.

"Yesterday evening Charles called at my apartment. I had thought at first he wanted a bed for the night, but it appears there was little need. Annabel would forgive his indiscretion if he accepted her father's proposition."

"Which was?" Kate questioned.

"To become the full-time legal advisor for his father-in-law's company. Oh, Charles is fully aware that the old fellow just wants him close at hand to keep an eye on him. And living together as they all do at Gresham House it will be a case of twenty-four hour surveillance.

Nonetheless, it's a situation Charles is willing to accept, though he assures me that if things become too difficult he will opt out of the legal profession altogether."

"And do what exactly?" Kate exclaimed.

"God knows," Edwin concluded, leaning forward and burying his head wearily into his hands.

"Oh my dear," Kate murmured consolingly, placing her hand lightly upon his back and stroking it in a comforting fashion. Edwin looked up and turned in his seat toward her.

"To burden you with such news before greeting you in a happier fashion is unforgivable." His grey eyes warmed to her flushed, delicate features and raising her chin with his hand, he kissed her warmly upon the lips. "Oh my dearest, how good it is to be back in the peace of Hengleford," he sighed. "The last few days in chambers have been fraught with difficulties of one kind or another."

"Come," Kate urged, rising from the couch and taking his hand in hers, "supper is ready. We will discuss the matter further when you have eaten." And with an encouraging smile she steered him through the doorway and down the hall into the dining room.

Although Edwin was reluctant to leave the comfort of the sitting room he was aware of her concern for his well-being and allowed himself to be led with good heart. Fortunately, once he had seated himself at the table and spied the game pie with all its trimmings, he embarked upon the meal with relish. He found time only to remark that he had not realized just how famished he had been.

Kate studied her husband's gradual unwinding with a smile of satisfaction. When their puddings had finally been devoured she suggested they might return to the cosiness of the sitting room with their coffee.

Should Charles persist in relinquishing his share of the business then there were decisions to be made. Could Edwin cope alone financially, Kate queried when they were seated. Or would his brother prefer perhaps to remain a sleeping partner, accepting increments on a regular basis. Unlike her contemporaries, Kate was well acquainted with such issues. Indeed, marriage to Edwin had taught her a great deal about money transactions and during the course of the evening, much to her husband's gratification, all possibilities concerning his predicament were aired in conversation.

Some six weeks later, Mr Andrew Forsyth, a reputable figure amongst the legal fraternity, took up his position at Jameson and Jameson. Whereupon Charles, having cleared his office of all personal items, vacated the premises. The parting of ways was an amicable one. Charles, having been well recompensed by his wealthy father-in-law for taking such steps, chose to remain a sleeping partner only, accepting a specified sum from the firm on a regular basis. From Edwin's point of view the agreement was most satisfactory, for he no longer had to find the initial wherewithal for his brother's share of the business and Jameson and Jameson remained to all intents and purpose a family concern.

The transition proved a successful one and despite Edwin's apprehension with regard to the newcomer, Andrew Forsyth was a conscientious worker and at forty years of age a devoted family man. Indeed, as colleagues they had much in common and between Monday and Thursday whilst Edwin resided in the city, they would on occasion, take a meal together at a nearby restaurant on a social footing.

Soon summer arrived, with its balmy days and long, light evenings. Amidst the neatly mowed lawns and large colourful gardens, the house at Longlea meadow took on a new dimension. In an effort to prepare a passable driveway, stones and rubble had bedded down nicely along the quarter mile track to reach the premises. The mud and grime that had been prevalent over the past few months had all but disappeared.

Little Edward's first birthday party, combined with Edwin's gave cause for elaborate celebrations. When Victoria and Reginald Hamilton, who had been staying in London, took the opportunity to surprise them with a visit, it was a time of happy reunion. Added to which, Kate was especially delighted to be able to repay the Hamilton's past kindness by inviting them to stay overnight in one of Longlea's five large, inviting bedrooms.

Indeed, as the family settled into a way of life that was both mentally stimulating and financially rewarding, Kate could find no justification for disrupting it. After so many half-hearted attempts to reveal her secret she concluded that she alone must carry the burden. All would have gone well perhaps, had not fate stepped in to deal an unexpected blow.

CHAPTER TEN

On Thursday morning, August the third, despite it being a working day, Andrew Forsyth remained at home nursing an extremely nasty attack of summer influenza. It was left to Edwin to deal with the workload on his behalf. It was at precisely that time, that young Doctor Smithson had been summoned to Jameson and Jameson solicitors in connection with a bequest from his late Aunt's will. At the appointed hour, Miss Bartholomew, prim and efficient as always, ushered the young man into Edwin's office and as the two men shook hands, they recognized each other from their consultation at the nearby hospital.

"I must apologize for my colleague's absence," Edwin began, "despite the warmth of the summer he is unfortunately beset by influenza. Please be seated. Miss. Bartholomew will bring you coffee whilst I fetch the necessary papers."

Murmuring sympathetically with regard to Mr Forsyth's condition, Doctor Smithson seated himself in the comfortable leather chair across from Edwin's desk. A moment later Edwin returned from the inner door with the relevant papers. Once the formalities were at an end the young doctor enquired in a friendly fashion as to the health of Kate and little Edward.

"Kate is remarkably fit," Edwin replied enthusiastically. "As for young Edward, despite his premature arrival, he has progressed extremely well."

Doctor Smithson credited himself with an excellent memory for the unusual and recalled the case to mind instantly. "Oh, a day or so early is nothing to worry about. As I recall, it was the circumstances surrounding his arrival that gave rise for concern, and a bad dose of jaundice to boot."

Edwin's smile diffused and his features grew taut as he hunched forward attentively over his desk. "But he was in the bay for premature babies," he stated earnestly.

"Ah, that was merely to keep an eye on the little chap, no? The shock to his system could have caused complication, but all turned out well in the end, did it not Sir?" The young man beamed, having made an obvious impression upon the older man for his swift recollection.

"Er. Yes of course." Edwin forced a smile.

The half-hour that followed with his client seemed like one of the longest Edwin had ever undertaken. He experienced a certain relief when the young man rose from his chair and finally departed. It was almost noon when Miss Bartholomew came in to fetch the post and she was surprised to find Edwin still seated at his desk. "Will there be anything else before you leave Mr Edwin?" she asked tentatively as she turned towards the door.

Edwin looked up from his desk, his face drawn and features ashen.

At once Miss Bartholomew thought he was ill and her voice trembled as she queried with concern. "Are you all right, Mr Edwin?"

"Mmm?" His grey eyes stared back at her with a vacant expression. Then, mindful of her query he answered, "A little weary Miss Bartholomew, that is all. I shall be off soon."

"Then have a good weekend, Sir."

"Thank you," Edwin replied flatly.

Throughout the journey homeward Edwin's mind was in turmoil. The knowledge that little Edward was not his child was a bitter blow. He loved the boy dearly. But that Kate had deceived him in so blatant a manner was totally unpardonable. His thoughts darted erratically from one past incident to another and, again and again, in a state of confusion, he revisited the time leading up to his proposal of marriage to Kate. It had been obvious from his first meeting with Kate at the farm, that she had formed an attachment for his brother, but that was over long since. Or was it, his conscience taunted.

Edwin's heart pounded and his hands felt clammy on the steering wheel. If the doctor's statement was correct and he had no reason to think otherwise, then the child was conceived weeks before their marriage. But Kate was on holiday with Dora at that time. She couldn't possibly... his body shuddered at the sudden recollection of her comment about seeing his brother. Charles, oh dear Lord, without doubt the boy belonged to Charles. Perchance, when Charles had learned of Kate's condition he had rejected her. Of course, that was it, for he was already committed to marrying Annabel. In truth, his own proposal must have seemed like a gift from heaven. The sudden realization that Kate and his own brother had allowed this ludicrous sham to continue made him feel physically sick. He abruptly pulled up at the roadside in order to remove himself from the car and inhale some fresh air.

It was almost eight o'clock in the evening when he drove up to Longlea Meadow. The feeling of utter defeat had left him. Now only anger remained as he stepped over the threshold.

Kate knew at once that something was amiss the moment Edwin entered the room, for his stance was defiant and his face ashen.

"By chance I met with young Doctor Smithson today," he remarked solemnly, observing her in a cool, clinical fashion as she rose from the deep cushioned sofa to greet him.

Kate's heart sank and her open arms fell loosely to her sides. Edwin had discovered her secret she could see the hurt in his steely grey eyes.

"Little Edward is my brother's child, is he not?" he stated forcefully.

Kate nodded, unable to speak.

"Both you and Charles must have been delighted at how easily I had been duped," Edwin continued wryly.

Kate shook her head. "Your brother knows nothing of the baby, Edwin. I give my word."

"YOUR WORD." Edwin exploded, backing away from her for fear he would strike out. "My brother's philandering has caused distress to many an innocent creature. Had you confided in me of your condition when I proposed, I would have wed you just the same. You see I loved you Kate, loved you deeply. Instead, you allowed me to think that you had begun to care for me and the pain caused by your deceit will stay with me always."

Tears welled in Kate's deep brown eyes. "I dared not speak of my doubts Edwin, for they were only doubts. And when little Edward was born and I knew the truth of it, I could not risk losing you."

"ME!" he raged, "OR A NAME FOR THE CHILD?"

For the first time since Kate had known him, she observed the full force of his wrath.

"That I have grown to love you deeply since our life together is…"Kate began quietly.

"Too late," Edwin interrupted sadly, turning his back on her and walking towards the large sash window overlooking the garden.

Amidst the deathly hush of the room Kate studied the rise and fall of his shoulders and agonized over any attempt she might make that would not meet with a rebuff.

Suddenly, with a look of grim determination upon his face Edwin turned towards her. "I have no wish to be the subject of ridicule, so I shall not disclose this matter to anyone, least of all Charles. To all concerned, the child is ours. And since you are so adept at concealing such matters, you should not find this task too difficult to accomplish," he added with contempt.

Kate opened her mouth to speak but he raised his hand to silence her. "I shall visit every other weekend, to keep abreast of little Edward's progress. As for you and I, our marriage is over. In future, I shall sleep in one of the guest rooms. Perhaps you will see to it that my clothes are moved accordingly."

Kate was aghast and looked at him in disbelief. "Edwin," she argued gently, "I love you more deeply than I ever imagined I could love anyone. I understand the terrible wrong that I have done in not revealing my suspicions at the onset. Misguidedly perhaps, I undertook the burden, but only because I loved you and wished to save you unnecessary anguish. Please, I beseech you, do not condemn me so readily." Her deep brown eyes brimmed with tears and Edwin was visibly moved by her plea.

Quietly he walked over the thick carpet towards the fireplace and resting his hands upon the wide mantle shelf stared in silence at the empty grate. Besieged by thoughts of all the happy times they had shared, he wanted to take her into his arms and close this terrible deception from his mind, but alas, taunting reminders of the day rallied forth to do battle with his sense of right and wrong. And as pride was the essence, he saw no satisfactory conclusion.

Mistakenly encouraged by his silence, Kate's outstretched hand rested gently upon his shoulder, "Come Edwin, you haven't eaten." She coaxed.

Scorn plagued his grey eyes as he swivelled on his heels to face her. "Perhaps you would bring me a tray. I'll be in the study," he remarked coldly, brushing passed her as he left the parlour.

Kate observed his departure with a consuming weariness. She had wrestled too often and too long with the guilt of the past and now her secret was out she experienced a modicum of relief. But alas, as one burden diminished so another took its place. Was life to continue in this manner she pondered. How much longer must she pay for her moment of imprudence? If Kate felt any strong emotion at all, it was a fleeting hatred of Charles. Charles who drifted in and out of relationships without thought for the chaos he created. Edwin also bore a portion of her dissatisfaction. For his love and devotion, as profound as he confessed it to be at the onset, was not sufficient to rise above this ordeal. A cry from the nursery brought her back to reality. After preparing Edwin's tray and taking it into the study, she made her way up the stairs to little Edward.

The following day Gerald Parkins called with the news that Britain had declared war on Germany. There had been rumours about the possibility for some months, but now the inevitable had happened and all were downcast at the news. Kate would like to have examined the consequences more fully with Edwin, but after a lengthy discussion with Gerald Parkins he offered his apologies and made ready to return earlier than anticipated to his chambers in London.

The first few weeks after their confrontation, Edwin visited the Longlea Meadow alternate weekends as promised. Throughout his stay Kate made every overture possible to redeem herself in her husband's eyes. But alas, Edwin was aloof and showed little interest in her well-being. He was civil in her company, but spoke little of his work at chambers. And despite Kate's attempts to draw him into conversation, he remained distant and uncommunicative. In truth, it was as if an invisible wall divided them.

Nonetheless, Edwin continued to lavish attention upon little Edward. And as the boy adored him, Kate accepted her own role with silent optimism. Friends knew nothing of the trauma, though on one occasion when Kate accompanied them both into the village, she was troubled that Gerald Parkins might suspect something was amiss. He eyed them with his usual perceptive manner and commented to Edwin that he was looking a little under the weather and hoped he wasn't over-taxing himself.

The doctor's observation was not far from the truth. Whilst Edwin stayed on in London, he spent most of the time at his desk in chambers, sifting through paper work and familiarizing himself with petty details that could well have been left to others in his employ. The truth of the matter was, Edwin found a certain solace in the sturdy oak panelled study surrounded by his reference books and portfolios. Indeed, it was a den in which to retreat until the festering of combat had healed.

Meanwhile, family outings to Hengleford and the surrounding villages took place so rarely that a charade on Kate and Edwin's part for the benefit of others proved unnecessary. However, it was a bizarre situation and in order to keep her sanity Kate became fully absorbed in household duties, farm business and the health of little Edward. All of which left little time to dwell upon the outcome of her unnatural marital status. Nonetheless, at close of day, when she sat by herself on the sitting room sofa, she likened the period to the first few months of Jack Pembleton's illness. In her private life she stood alone. The only difference since that time was that she was financially secure, but alas, the latter offered little consolation.

CHAPTER ELEVEN

It was a cold, crisp, November morning when Charles Jameson unexpectedly strolled into Edwin's office. "Good morning, brother. Forgive the intrusion, but I have booked us a table for lunch at Monsieur Jacques."

It was the first Edwin had seen of him for months. And now, knowing the truth of the matter concerning little Edward, he looked up from his desk and eyed his brother warily. "And if I have a previous engagement?" he queried grimly.

"Tut tut, picked a bad moment have I?" Charles quipped. "As for engagements, I checked earlier with Miss Bartholomew. You have none." His lips curled in a smug smile as he seated himself in the leather chair opposite.

"Charles, I have much work and positively no inclination for a battle of words," Edwin concluded, returning his gaze to the letters upon his desk.

"Then make an exception today, as a farewell gesture to your kith and kin before he leaves the shores of this scepter'd isle," Charles retorted wryly.

Edwin sensed an air of impending doom and a sudden dread. Had Kate confessed to Charles that the child was his? This prompted him to raise his head and take note. "Farewell? What are you talking about?" he queried cautiously.

"I have had my fill of old man Soames," Charles began in a disgruntled fashion. "He consistently goes against my advice, crushes my enthusiasm and puts me down to boot."

Relief flooded Edwin's being. "Have you spoken to Annabel?" he sighed, placing his pen into the narrow channel of the ink stand in front of him.

"Annabel. Bah, she agrees with daddy every time old boy. Her lavish wardrobe depends upon it."

"If things are as bad as you say, Annabel would support you, I am sure."

"Support," Charles scoffed, "from Annabel? My dear brother, not all are fortunate enough to be part-nered by a wife like yours."

Edwin winced. "What are you going to do?"

"I shall reveal all over lunch," Charles replied, swiv-elling in his chair and eyeing the large, round clock upon the wall. "Now, it is almost twelve o'clock, our taxi will be waiting," he concluded rising to his feet.

Although Edwin had no desire to leave the comfort of his chambers, curiosity got the better of him. With some misgivings he reached for his overcoat and traced his brother's footsteps. It was Edwin's first visit to the restaurant in Hislop Lane since his marriage to Kate yet, despite the time lapse he found the place had lost none of its charm. Lighted candles set in dark empty wine bottles stood like miniature beacons upon the red and white chequered cloths covering the generous circum-ferences of the tables. The sight generated such a warm welcome that the starkness of the November day was soon forgotten.

Charles and Edwin removed their overcoats and made their way to a corner table. This cued the overly fed patron who had been biding his time behind a well-stocked bar at the far end of the room, to step forth and greet them. Monsieur Jacques never forgot a face. Indeed, he was renowned for this particular accomplishment and at recognition of the brothers, his robust features gave way to a generous smile. After a jovial rebuke to Edwin for not yet having brought his bride to sample their famous fare, he handed them two large boldly printed menus. Then, fingering his lengthy moustache that curled upwards at the edges in a comical fashion, departed for their aperitifs.

Whilst waiting for their drinks the bell above the door signalled the arrival of regular clientele and soon the premises began to throb with activity. From his seat in the corner, Edwin studied the wide oak beams that stretched the length of the low slung ceiling. His gaze continued to the pictures and mementoes of France clinging limpet fashion to the white washed walls. Inevitably he was reminded of happier times with Kate and a faraway look appeared in his grey eyes at recollection of their honeymoon in Paris. Suddenly his brother's voice invaded his reverie and though he felt somewhat thwarted by the intrusion, he reluctantly directed his thoughts to the realities of the day.

"You and I have neglected each other of late, I fear, dear brother," Charles stated whimsically, peering over the top of his menu. He studied Edwin from across the table. Despite the smile that accompanied his words, Edwin detected a note of regret in his voice. He was surprised by it. They had never been especially close and since Charles had played a major role in turning his own world upside down, he had often of late despised his very existence. Nonetheless, the adage that blood is thicker than water prevailed, and now, in a curious way he felt responsible for his brother's lack of stability. Had he been more of a guide and mentor after the devastating loss of their parents, perhaps Charles would have behaved differently.

"I've accepted several new clients since your departure so my work load has increased somewhat," he remarked apologetically, "but doubtless Soames has kept you extremely active also."

Charles grimaced. "Day and night. But not for much longer, old boy." An amused look fired the deep blue of his eyes and his dark handsome features took on an air of satisfaction.

At that moment a waiter approached and set their drinks upon the table. "We shall toast my new vocation," Charles announced dramatically, raising his glass.

"Which is?" Edwin quizzed, studying his companion's face intently.

"I have offered my services to…" Charles hesitated, delaying the outcome in a teasing manner, "the government."

"In what capacity?" Edwin asked, leaning forward and awaiting his explanation with interest.

"As a member of the Armed Forces. I embark on this new…"

"The Armed Forces," Edwin broke in, aghast at the prospect, "but what on earth possessed you to do such a thing?"

Charles raised his hand to silence the interruption. "I have all the necessary qualifications and as I was about to say, will be embarking on this new venture as a non-commissioned officer on the fifth of December." He beamed.

"My God," Edwin gasped, his face paling under the candle's glow. "You know that Kitchener's preparing for a lengthy war? Already there have been two major battles at Marne and Ypres with considerable loss of life."

"Precisely, old chap," Charles pulled a face. "A fine opportunity, don't you think, to put my hunting and shooting skills to the test?"

"War is not a game, Charles," Edwin exclaimed, looking decidedly perplexed.

"No?" Charles raised his eyebrows in the query.

"No" Edwin insisted, "and what does Annabel think?"

"My dear fellow, Annabel doesn't think. Other than remarking that the uniform will enhance my physique, the whole account is beyond her comprehension."

Edwin shook his head in exasperation.

"Come," Charles urged, anxious to sample his Dubonnet, "raise your glass and wish me well."

Reluctantly, Edwin's fingers closed around the aperitif at his side. It was apparent from the look of defiance upon his brother's face that there was little he could do to dissuade him from this course of action.

"To me then," Charles coaxed, raising his glass in salute. After sipping a little of the liquid, he suggested a further toast. " To you and Katherine. May your life together continue to be a happy one, blessed with a host of offspring."

"What prompts your remark about offspring?"

"Well, you have one boy have you not? It would be a lonely life for the little fellow without the companionship of others," Charles concluded innocently as the waiter approached with their first course.

"You have never visited Longlea have you?" Edwin remarked tentatively.

"No, nor do I wish to," his brother stated flatly as he sampled his pate.

Edwin looked up from his plate in surprise. "Why not?"

"The mere sight of such perfect domesticity would undoubtedly make me envious, added to which I do not think Katherine would approve of such an invitation."

Edwin winced again at his reference to Kate. "What makes you say that?" he asked, pursing his lips in indignation.

"Do not misunderstand me, brother," Charles remarked hastily. "Your wife is an admirable lady, but on the occasion I met her at the station to whisk her back to your chambers she enthused so much about what a wonderful chap you were I felt quite jaded by the experience."

Edwin's face coloured in embarrassment. "Jesting apart," he urged.

"No jest, I swear it," Charles sighed. "And she saw fit to bruise my ego to boot."

"Your ego?" Edwin queried attentively.

"Despite her appealing softness, she has an incredibly forthright manner. I cannot remember her exact words, but she put me firmly in my place," Charles stated glibly. "Suffice to say though," he continued, musing ruefully upon the occasion, "if she were mine, the Monarch would have one less volunteer in his army today."

"Can you not be serious for a moment." Edwin muttered irritably.

"Oh, but I am my dear fellow. I have never been more so." Charles's deep blue eyes looked at him directly and there was a tinge of regret in his voice. "Now, shall we delay this cross examination and proceed with lunch in a more amiable fashion?" A smile of encouragement spread across his face tempering the brusqueness of his statement and before Edwin could acknowledge him, the waiter approached with the main course.

For the first time in many weeks Edwin studied his dinner plate with relish. As he pondered upon his brother's remarks, a tremendous relief flooded his being. He knew Charles well enough by now to suspect that he had made further advances to Kate, but joy of joys, by his own admission she would have none of it. In truth, the knowing of it sent his mind agog with pleasure. All this time he had thought Kate was still enamoured by his brother. Now, to discover that she was not, was a most uplifting experience. In the half hour that followed Charles continued to ramble on excitedly about the advantages of his new career and though Edwin was attentive at first, he soon found himself distracted by plans of his own to return to Longlea meadow. Presently he directed his gaze to the clock upon the wall, whereupon his brother's voice broke into his reverie.

"Are my revelations becoming something of a bore brother?" Charles retorted, slightly rattled by his companion's obvious lack of interest.

"No, not at all," Edwin replied apologetically, "but I do have some paperwork to attend to by three o'clock."

"Then we must order dessert at once. I can't have you neglecting business matters too long, after all, my lucrative income still depends upon it," Charles scoffed.

Despite his brother's shortcomings, Edwin felt a sudden need to make amends. "Charles I do wish you well," he insisted benevolently, "and perhaps when you have leave, we can meet up here at Monsieur Jacques."

Charles looked at him with a quizzical expression upon his face. "We shall see."

It was almost two o'clock when together they rose from the table and reached for their coats. As a farewell gesture, Edwin insisted on paying the bill and moved over to the proprietor who was standing behind the bar. Charles, having spotted an old acquaintance seated at the other side of the room, took the opportunity to present himself. When Charles finally returned to his brother's side, Edwin and Monsieur Jacques were deep in conversation.

"Sorry to interrupt but you did want to return to chambers before three," he broke in, hastily buttoning his overcoat.

With a friendly smile the proprietor handed Edwin one of his elaborate business cards. Then, with a hasty farewell, the brothers departed for the nearest taxi rank.

"I'll drop you off first," Charles insisted. "There are a few things I have to do before returning home."

"Why not come into chambers? Miss Bartholomew would be only too happy to make you coffee if you have the time," Edwin suggested, all too aware that several months might pass before they would meet again.

"What's this old chap?" Charles grinned. "A sudden attack of brotherly concern?"

At that moment the taxi they were in came to a standstill and Edwin alighted. "For whatever reason," he replied solemnly as he turned and held out his hand, "the very best of luck to you. Take good care."

Charles slid along the leather seat towards the open door and moved by his genuine concern, clasped Edwin's outstretched hand. "I will brother, I promise."

It was almost a quarter to three in the afternoon before Edwin finally walked over the threshold of his outer office. His mood was one of cordial optimism and on approaching Miss Bartholomew's desk he extended a friendly greeting and asked her to join him with his list of engagements. No sooner had he removed his overcoat and seated himself in readiness than the prim figure of his secretary appeared in the doorway.

"I shall be leaving for Hengleford shortly," he announced. "Tell me what..."

"But it is Wednesday, Sir." Miss Bartholomew's thick dark eyebrows arched with surprise and behind the magnification of heavy rimmed spectacles her green eyes clouded with concern. "There is nothing amiss I hope."

"On the contrary, Miss Bartholomew," Edwin beamed reassuringly, "everything is extremely satisfactory. Nonetheless, I wish to delay any further appointments until Tuesday of next week. May I leave that task in your capable hands?"

"Of course, Mr Edwin. I shall notify your clients at once," she acknowledged. "Will that be all Sir?" she concluded efficiently.

"Any letters to sign?" he asked as he reached for the attaché case on the floor at his side.

"Only two. I'll fetch them immediately."

Edwin glanced up as she moved towards the door. "Oh, Mr Forsyth is out at present," he remarked as an afterthought. "Will you apologize for my sudden departure and ask him to telephone me at home if he is in difficulty?"

In polite response Miss Bartholomew gave a courteous nod of her head and with the appointment book clutched firmly to her flat bosom left the room, closing the door quietly behind her.

After her departure Edwin rose from his swivel chair and moved towards the window. In a dubious fashion he viewed the overcast skies and pondered upon his best course of action. The morning paper had predicted atrocious weather for the evening and despite his wish to return to Longlea meadow as soon as possible, he had no desire to cover the distance by motor car if there was a more satisfactory alternative. Turning from the window he paced the length of the room and with a look of determination upon his face removed the current Bradshaw from the bookshelf. On searching swiftly through the pages, he discovered that the 5.55pm from St. Pancras to Hengleford was the only train that would get him home this evening. Alas, it was a slow one, stopping at several stations en route he noted glumly. However, on the brighter side, on arrival perhaps the stationmaster would oblige him with transport of some kind. Glancing up at the large, round clock attached to the oak panelled wall, he noted it was already 4.25pm. Moving briskly to his desk he flicked the switch of the extension speaker. "Miss Bartholomew?" he queried hurriedly.

"Yes, Mr Edwin?"

"Would you come into my office?"

The request prompted a swift response from the puzzled Miss Bartholomew and a moment later she tapped his door and stepped over the threshold. Edwin looked up from the scattered paper work upon his desk.

"Would you arrange for a taxi to take me to St. Pancras at a quarter past five? And also for one of the porters to drive my vehicle to Glapthorn Motors on the Chingford Road? Here are the keys." Edwin stated, removing them from his trouser pocket and placing them into the palm of her hand. "Oh, and be sure whoever takes it asks the proprietor to service the motor and keep it under cover until my return next week. Give the porter some petty cash for his return journey."

Despite a speedy conclusion to business it was already dark when Edwin finally left chambers. Nonetheless, as he sat in the taxi bound for the station, his heart warmed to the prospect of three or four free days in which to attempt to make his peace with Kate. Indeed, such was his preoccupation, that when he alighted from the cab and began to cross the busy pavement to the station gates, he was oblivious to the fall of snow that had begun in earnest.

Chapter Twelve

A splendid looking grandfather clock stood on the mosaic tiled floor at the far end of the spacious hallway at Longlea. Its dulcet tones struck seven o'clock as Mrs Porter, having stayed an hour longer than usual to finish her chores, gave a cheery farewell to Kate and departed. Kate observed little Edward sleeping peacefully in his bed, then returned to the warmth of the sitting room. There, amidst the homely scattering of objet d'art she settled by the fire with a supper tray resting on the small circular table at her side.

Today she was overly weary. Apart from a short trip by pony and trap into the village with Albert earlier, much of her day had been devoted to book keeping, an exhaustive task at the best of times. Since the acquisition of Josiah Tebbutt's land and his modest flock of sheep, there seemed a never-ending volume of tasks and official papers demanding attention. The two hands she employed from the nearby village of Washbrook had turned out to be well versed with regard to shepherding and indeed they worked hard without instruction. Nonetheless, Albert had not been in the best of health for some time and was now carrying out lighter duties. This resulted in a great deal of extra work being placed on young Ted's shoulders. Although willing to take on a greater load, Kate thought it would be unfair to take advantage of his bigheartedness for too lengthy a time.

As the weeks passed by it was clear she would need to take on at least one extra hand. In the past she would have talked the matter over with Edwin and together they would have arrived at a suitable solution. But once again, she sighed, the problem was hers and hers alone to deal with.

It had been a depressing time of late, with the constant talk of war and how soon the able -bodied young men of the village would be departing to do their bit for King and country. Some of the lads who had barely left school were keen to enlist in Kitchener's Army. Indeed, their eyes lit up at the mere mention of it. The prospect of visiting a foreign land, far away from the tranquil area of Hengleford, appeared something of an adventure.

In the normal course of things Kate welcomed any distraction from personal matters. However, with the anniversary of her wedding day fast approaching her mind began to wander. She could concentrate on little else but her past actions concerning Edwin. Was it so wrong of her at the onset not to have mentioned even the possibility of a child? To have avoided causing hurt when perhaps there was no necessity for it? Or was the latter merely a lame excuse on her part to avoid disclosure of her impropriety?

A barrage of silent reproach overwhelmed her, prompting doubts as to the limits of her own integrity. For in hindsight, had she known with certainty she was carrying Charles' child, would she have had sufficient will power to reject Edwin's proposal? The outcome of such hypothetical meanderings left her feeling more desolate than ever and rising from her chair she picked up the poker and prodded aimlessly at the burning coals of the fire.

In truth, the knowledge that little Edward was not Edwin's child had been as much of a trauma for her as it was for her husband. But she loved Edwin deeply and by way of atonement would have carried the burden of deceit to her grave to save him unnecessary heartache. What a paradox it was she ruminated. Edwin doted on the boy yet spurned the perpetrator of the child's existence. An aura of gloom and despondency descended as Kate replaced the poker in its stand and stepped backwards into the comfort of her seat.

Suddenly she looked across at her husband's fireside chair and as she mused upon the day of its purchase, her deep, brown eyes grew bright with recall. Such pains had been taken to ensure his comfort and the leather winged chair she had chosen had gained his wholehearted approval. Of course similar efforts had gone into furnishing the rest of the house, but no response from Edwin had been more gratifying than the subject of his chair. Moments of trivia paraded before her mind's eye and when eventually Kate returned her gaze to the flames of the fire, her bosom heaved with a sigh of unhappiness.

Edwin was innately forthright, the epitome of truthfulness. Her behaviour had prompted deception of a most cruel nature. If only he would allow her to make amends and give her time to reassure him of her love. Alas, however, such hopes appeared without foundation. For with each visit his cool response towards her thwarted any opportunity for reconciliation. Dear God, how could she have jeopardized the only happiness she had truly known?

At precisely quarter past nine in the evening the telephone bell in Edwin's study rang out. Its shrillness echoed through the silent house, startling Kate momentarily.

Quickly she gathered her thoughts and raising her lengthy skirt, hurried across the hallway. The study door was open and moving over to the wall by the mahogany desk she unhooked the receiver from its clip. It was the elderly Miss Phipps, who was employed by the post office to work the tiny exchange. "I have Doctor Parkin's wife on the line for you Mrs Jameson," she announced.

A distorted crackle preceded the familiar voice of Dora. "I must apologize for disturbing you at this late hour Katherine, but I thought you should know that the men are likely to be late for work in the morning. There has been an accident on the main railway line just outside Hengleford. Ted, Albert and a few others from the village have gone with Gerald to offer assistance."

"It's kind of you to telephone Dora, but how awful about the accident. What on earth could have …"

"A derailment was mentioned," Dora interrupted, "but that is only hearsay. Nonetheless it's a fearful night for any mishap, still snowing heavily."

"Albert predicted as much. Fortunately we took his advice and prepared the barns in readiness yesterday. Thankfully, all the animals are under cover," Kate replied.

"A wise action. Now my dear, I shall do my utmost to be with you around half past eight in the morning, as Mrs Porter may well be involved in looking after her own family. Her elder son William as you know works for the London Midland and is usually homeward bound on the 5.55 from St. Pancras."

Kate sucked in her breath. "I had no idea. How dreadful. Let us hope that the accident is not as serious as it is rumoured."

"Indeed," Dora reiterated hopefully.

"As to the other matter of you footing it here in the morning Dora, please don't bother. I shall manage perfectly well. Little Edward can accompany me on my tasks."

"Oh no Katherine," Dora exclaimed, aghast at the thought. "There could be dangerous drifts across the meadow and I should have no peace of mind thinking of you both. No, please, wait until I arrive."

"Very well," Kate conceded with a smile, "but do take care on your walk from the village."

"I shall and now before I attend to other chores I'll leave you with thoughts on a lighter matter," Dora continued. "Have you and Edwin made plans for your wedding anniversary? I ask, because Gerald and I would be more than willing to look after Edward should the need arise. Failing that, we should like to prepare a meal for you both by way of celebration."

Kate hesitated. The gesture was a generous one and she had no wish to belittle it. In so far as she could tell, her dear friends were unaware of any difficulties between Edwin and herself. However, with any length of time spent in close proximity, their relationship would be open to scrutiny and nothing would escape the perceptiveness of Gerald Parkins. "As yet Edwin has said nothing with regard to the occasion, or of any special arrangements having been made," Kate replied cautiously.

"Then perhaps you could quiz him at an opportune moment," Dora suggested cheerfully. "And now I really must away and prepare a flask of hot drink in readiness for Gerald's return."

"Thank you again for calling Dora," Kate concluded appreciatively. "And I look forward to seeing you in the morning."

After placing the receiver securely in its stand Kate wandered over to the study window and parting the rich velvet curtains peered out over the garden. The area was a carpet of white. From the light over the barn that housed the generator she could see it was still snowing heavily. Dora was right she pondered ruefully. It was a dreadful night for any mishap to occur and any help at the scene would be severely handicapped by such wintry conditions. She shivered momentarily, then, drawing the curtains to a close, made her way back to the warmth of the sitting room.

By now the pot of tea on her tray was cold and the remaining sandwiches on the china plate curled unappetizingly at the edges. It occurred to her she might retire early but her mind rebelled. For reflective indulgences throughout the evening had created a restless feeling within and she knew she would not sleep. Reluctantly, she left the warmth of the fireside and entered the hall en route to the large kitchen. She would heat up some milk, she mused and take it back to the sitting room.

The train grinded to a halt. As the sound of chatter and banging of doors echoed through the carriages, Edwin rubbed his hand over the compartment window and peered out anxiously at the snow covered platform. The tiny outlying station afforded little protection for travellers and those alighting from the train pulled up their coat collars to shield themselves against the wind before hurrying towards the exit. He had been wise to leave his vehicle in London, Edwin reflected. Goodness knows what difficulties might have arisen had he travelled by road. Leaning forward, he removed his watch from his waistcoat pocket and studied it under the dimly lit bulb. Half past eight. Save further delays, Hengleford was but twenty minutes away. Replacing the time piece into the safety of his pocket, he rested back in his seat and tapped his fingers impatiently on the arm rest. The journey had been an incredibly tedious one, with drifts of snow on the track causing numerous interruptions. Indeed, over the last hour they had continued at no more than a snail's pace. A sensible precaution no doubt, but irritating nonetheless. Suddenly the piercing shrill of the guard's whistle invaded the night air. As the engine gathered momentum and the monotonous rocking of the carriage began, Edwin considered the task ahead.

By the time he had arranged transport to Hengleford and arrived at Longlea meadow, the hour would be late. Would Kate have retired to her bed, he reflected. It was a disappointing prospect, for he had thought to attempt a reunion that very evening. With unseeing eyes he stared at his reflection in the elongated window and began to ponder philosophically upon his own obstinacy. It had been a bitter blow to learn that Edward was not his child, but in hindsight, he had solved nothing by his initial outburst. And later he had worsened matters by remaining uncommunicative. Throughout their periods of separation he had spent hours ruminating upon Kate's lack of discretion until finally, all the rage and humiliation experienced at the onset was tempered by compassion.

He was not a pious man, but in a strange, inexplicable way, his own anguish had prompted a greater understanding of her impropriety. He knew that in the past she had suffered unspeakable hardship at the hands of Jack Pembleton. In such a climate she would have been easy prey for someone like Charles, well versed in the way of women. That his brother now or ever had been a threat to his marriage was a fear unfounded, and the realization of such news prompted a jubilation he had not felt in months. There was much to do to make amends, for alas so much time in their lives had been wasted. Indeed, time enough for Kate to have resigned herself to his disinterest and have made plans of her own, his conscience taunted. His stomach knotted with apprehension. Such a possibility had not occurred to him until now and the mere notion of it sent a chill of fear trickling down his spine.

By way of easing his uncertainty he drew momentary comfort from the fact that he had experienced few cases of the fairer sex wishing to divorce their husbands. Indeed, most married women relied on their partners for their livelihood and resigned themselves to imperfect situations. But Kate was not like most women. She had the will, the funds and a capacity for striking out on her own, in part, qualities of independence that had endeared her to him at the onset. Dear God, he lamented, had he come to his senses too late. Before Edwin could ruminate further, the sound of the engine's brakes being applied shattered the night air and the seat beneath him began to vibrate in a frightening manner. The compartment around him gave an almighty groan and suddenly the whole carriage, having wrenched free of its couplings, careered along the embankment and rolled over on to its side. At which point Edwin found himself propelled helplessly towards the window opposite.

Chapter Thirteen

When Kate stirred from her chair to place the mesh guard in front of the dying embers of the fire, she glanced at the clock on the mantle-piece and was aghast to discover it was almost eleven o'clock. An early start was required of her in the morning and she had not intended to retire to bed quite so late. However, the hot drink combined with the heat of the fire had played their part in easing her restlessness and now she viewed the prospect of sleep with relish. She was about to switch off the lights in the sitting room when she heard the sound of voices outside. Skirting around the furniture she hurried into the hall. Suddenly the bell rang and there was an urgent knocking on the door. Once opened, the snow covered figures of Albert and Gerald Parkins came into view and at once she ushered them inside. Both were grateful for the flow of warmth from within the house and as they stepped in unison over the threshold Doctor Parkins removed his black felt trilby and ran his fingers through his dishevelled white hair.

"Katherine my dear, I know the hour is late," he began apologetically, "but would you fetch pillows and blankets and do your best to make a comfortable bed upon your couch in the sitting room."

It was a curious request and concern showed itself upon her face. But she nodded her head in understanding and was about to proceed when she noted dark stains that looked like blood upon his overcoat.

Gerald Parkins looked at her directly, his tired, blue eyes tracing her stare. He would have wished to have broken the news more gently, but alas, there was little time for formalities. "Please hurry Katherine, Edwin is in the car," he stated calmly, "and when Albert and I bring him into the house I want him kept as warm and comfortable as possible."

Kate's eyebrows arched in surprise, "Edwin," she gasped in horror, "but what has happened? Has he been taken ill?"

Events of the evening had begun to take their toll and for that reason the doctor's retort bore a hint of impatience. "Hasten with your preparations my dear and I shall enlighten you in due course."

Distress inched its way over Kate's features and in a somewhat bemused state she hurried up the stairs to the linen cupboard. She gathered blankets and a pillow and then quickly returned to the sitting room to prepare the makeshift bed as requested.

"Come then Albert," Gerald turned to his companion, "we must get our patient out of the car and into the warmth as soon as possible." Before departing he called out to Kate to prepare a bowl of hot water and some fresh towels.

After the men had departed Kate hurried up to Edwin's room for his pyjamas and thick plaid dressing gown and returning to the sitting room placed them on one of the fireside chairs. Then she hurried into the kitchen, filled a bowl with hot water, fetched fresh towels from the cupboard and setting them on a small trolley normally used for high tea, wheeled it through for convenience. Having spied that the fire was almost out she quickly set about reviving it and was relieved when finally the new wood took hold and bright yellow flames leapt up the chimney. With the bustle of hasty preparations over, the room took on an aura of ominous expectancy. Kate stared into the brightness of the fire and her head buzzed with a stream of hypothesizes. What had been the purpose of Edwin's unexpected journey? Had he come to a decision about their relationship that would not keep until the following week? Had his motor vehicle been in an accident? On tenterhooks she stood by the couch awaiting his appearance.

Finally the men appeared, hands linked, carrying Edwin chair fashion over the threshold of the room. As Kate observed the thick, coarse blanket covering his head and the numerous cuts and bruises upon his face, her heart went out to him. His trousers were torn and bloodied, the left leg swathed in bandages. Beneath the overcoat that was draped about his shoulders his left arm hung limply at his side.

"Oh my dear," Kate's voice trembled with emotion as she moved towards him, "what on earth has happened?" She thought she detected a look of relief in Edwin's bleary, grey eyes, but before he could respond he began to shiver violently.

"Your questions will all be answered in good time Katherine," Gerald Parkins interrupted in a kindlier tone. "Now my dear, whilst Albert and I clean Edwin up a little and get him into his night attire would you be so kind as to attend to some hot tea? Though first I would welcome the use of your medicine chest, as I have run short of lint and would appreciate it if you have some to spare."

"I already have the kettle on the stove," she replied as she made her way towards the door.

"I'll build up the fire whilst your gone Missus," Albert offered gently, folding his cap and putting it in his pocket.

Kate gave him a look of gratitude before leaving the room. "Thank you Albert."

At once Albert slipped out of his snow covered coat. After relieving the doctor of his outer attire he carried the items through to the hall and hung them on the large coat stand. On return he quickly backed up the fire, which by now was giving out sufficient heat and marched through to the kitchen to wash the coal dust from his hands.

Kate prepared a second bowl of hot water whilst the menfolk then set about the task of getting Edwin out of his torn and bloodied clothing. This was difficult to achieve without causing distress for every muscle in the patient's body ached and his movements were extremely limited. For much of the time Edwin bore the pain in silence though on occasion, when it was extreme he let it be known.

"My dear fellow," Gerald Parkins chided softly as he used the last of his antiseptic lotion to clean the wounds upon Edwin's face, "had you heeded my advice and been admitted to the County hospital overnight, they could have done far more than I to relieve your discomfort."

Despite his unease, Edwin would have none of it. "My need to be home was most pressing Gerald," he winced stubbornly.

"Well, the nurse here at Longlea will no doubt be a more agreeable sight to you than any at the hospital," the doctor concluded with a smile as Kate re-entered with the tea tray.

At which point Albert made to leave. "If you don't need me any more gentlemen, I'll be on my way. It's late and the missus will be fretting," he commented, edging towards the sitting room door.

"I'll be going myself shortly Albert," the doctor said as he secured the last of the bandages and closed his bag. "Will you not stay for a cup of tea and take advantage of a lift home?"

"Thank you all the same doctor, but if you don't mind I'll be moving on. Take good care, Mr Edwin." His eyes glanced fleetingly at Edwin before opening the door.

Gerald Parkins nodded his head in understanding. Albert's willingness to assist him throughout the whole of the evening had been most commendable but he was no longer a young man and weariness etched itself upon his features. "Sleep well then Albert and thank you for all your assistance."

Kate placed the fresh pot of tea upon a nearby table and as she accompanied Albert through the hallway to the coat stand she squeezed his arm affectionately. "You had forgotten your torch, Albert," she said, handing it to him. "And thank you again for all your help. Without you, I..." Lost for words her deep, brown eyes brimmed with gratitude.

Albert shifted uncomfortably under the hall light. "It's nothing. Just hope Mr Edwin has a good kip. It'll do wonders, you'll see. Speaking of sleep, I won't be up too early but I'll get hold of Archie and a couple of other lads to help us out for a day or two," he remarked as he donned his overcoat and cap. "Don't worry though." he added moving sideways through the half open doorway.

In all the confusion Kate had forgotten Dora's telephone call until this moment. Was it possible that the derailment was connected with Edwin's plight? "Albert, Master Edwin wasn't on the train was he?" she queried in a whisper of uncertainty.

"Aye." Her foreman nodded glumly.

Kate caught her breath, "And Mrs Porter's boy, William?" her voice echoed.

Albert's stomach churned as the scene of the accident sprang vividly to mind. "The lad's gone, I'm sorry to say. A sad business," he stated wearily.

Kate's relief at Edwin's safety was suddenly tempered by the fate of Mrs Porter's elder son. "How awful, poor Mrs Porter," she murmured sympathetically. "I shall visit at the first opportunity and please tell Ted that I understand he will be needed at home for the next few days."

"You're going to have your hands full for a bit," Albert insisted as he pulled the peak of his cap low down over his forehead. "Like I say, don't worry. I'll give her your sympathy and explain things." Then, clutching his coat collar close about his neck he gave a hasty farewell and turned on his heels.

Kate watched for a moment as his footsteps traced the light of his torch over the snow covered pathway. Then, shivering at the intrusion of cold air, she quickly closed the front door and made her way back to the sitting room. Albert's news with regard to Mrs Porter's boy was uppermost in her mind and the trauma of it showed upon her face as she re-entered the room and approached the couch where Edwin lay. Gerald Parkins stood with his back to the fire and observed her movements with his perceptive blue eyes.

"You must forgive me if I appeared a little brusque earlier my dear," he announced apologetically. "I should have wished to have prepared you in some way for the entrance of this sorry sight," he continued with a light hearted gesture towards Edwin, "but alas, time was of the essence."

Kate studied her husband's features and relaxed a little for the colour in his cheeks had returned. And as his body responded to the heat of the fire he no longer shook in that uncontrollable fashion. With a hint of a smile she turned her gaze to the elderly doctor who, by now, was looking decidedly weary.

"I understand," she acknowledged. "This evening must have been a dreadful ordeal. Dora telephoned me earlier with suspicions of a derailment though until Albert informed me just now I had no idea Edwin's plight was connected to it."

"Mmm," Gerald Parkins nodded as he turned sideways to the fire and warmed his hands by its glow. "Albert spoke of Mrs Porter's boy then?" he questioned softly.

"Only after I had enquired about him," Kate replied.

"A tragedy," he remarked sadly, shaking his head. "Alas one feels impotent in the midst of so much despair." A look of grief pervaded his tired, blue eyes and in a momentary lapse of confidence, his spirit waned. "Indeed, on occasions such as these, I wish I had sought a different profession."

"Well I for one am most grateful that you did not," Kate offered reassuringly. "And there are many in the village who have reason to think likewise," she concluded as she rose from her chair and made her way over to the tea tray.

Her movement dispersed the doctor's reverie. "No more for me my dear," he remarked glancing at the clock on the mantle-piece. "Good heavens it is almost one o'clock. I must be on my way. Dora will be anxious for news."

"Ah," Kate uttered as she recalled her friend's willingness to visit in the early hours. "Dora has offered to entertain little Edward later this morning whilst I attend to farm chores but under the circumstances do try to dissuade her."

A look of amusement spread across the doctor's face relaxing the tautness of his features. "You know Dora, my dear. If she has promised to assist you then there is little I can say that will persuade her otherwise."

"I'll leave the matter to your discretion," Kate yielded with a smile.

"As for our patient, I have left this sleeping draught," Gerald stated, pointing to a small packet he had placed on the mantle-piece earlier. "It should offer Edwin some relief in the early hours. Also, when it's convenient my dear, perhaps you could light a fire in your bedroom and when I visit later this afternoon, we can together assist him up the stairs. For the present however, he is fairly at ease upon the couch and as a warm environment is of the utmost importance, the appropriate place for him is here beside the fire."

Gerald Parkins picked up his bag and moving over to the couch rested the back of his hand momentarily upon Edwin's brow. "You will most certainly be stiff and uncomfortable for some time to come my dear fellow. But continued warmth and rest will allay any serious consequences. Indeed, though it may not feel like it, you are a very lucky man." Edwin raised his good hand and when the doctor took it into his own he thanked him for his concern. "You will I take it, have the good sense to do as your nurse orders," Gerald quantified with a smile.

Edwin nodded accordingly whereupon the elderly doctor moved quietly across the carpeted floor towards the door. Kate followed him through to the hallway. As he donned his overcoat and hat, he looked at her directly. "A word of warning Katherine. Edwin's body has suffered a tremendous shock, which in turn could cause complications. So should anything untoward occur please telephone me at once."

Alarm swept over Kate's face at the seriousness of his tone. "But, but he will be all right?"

"Of course, my dear. Most of his injuries are superficial. As for the rest, they will heal in due course," he answered, bending forward and squeezing her cheek with his hand reassuringly. "I merely mentioned the latter as a precaution. Now, Dora is arriving at eight or thereabouts you say. Well I shall see you mid-afternoon, so for the present my dear, adieu." Placing a light kiss upon her forehead, he withdrew a flashlight from his overcoat pocket and promptly departed. Whereupon Kate bolted the door behind him.

But for the odd comment, Edwin had spoken little throughout the previous hour. As Kate moved back into the sitting room to tend to his needs, she was conscious of the fact that this was the first time they had been alone since his arrival. His tired, grey eyes observed her as she entered the room and although his physical distress was apparent, she had no notion of his true feelings. Until now her own emotions had been curbed by the physical effort of attending to the needs of others.

But in the stillness of the room, the knowledge that her husband could so easily have been another victim of the train disaster was a disturbing realization. As the strain released itself her hands began to shake and in order to disguise her distress she made her way over to the grate to replenish the fire. Edwin lay upon the couch a few feet behind her and as she knelt at the hearth she felt his eyes upon her.

"Kate," his voice was but a whisper and when she turned to face him she could barely suppress the tears in her deep, brown eyes. His left arm, now freshly bandaged, rested in a sling across his chest whilst the other stretched out toward her. She reached for it cautiously.

"I know you must be overly weary my dear," he murmured, "but please sit with me a moment."

His plea was a simple one but it moved her to the extreme. And yet, even as Kate rested upon the edge of the couch, she could not rid herself of this sense of foreboding.

Still his hand clutched hers. "In truth, I do not know where to..." he broke off briefly, in an effort to ease his back against the pillows.

"Hush then my dearest," she cooed in a maternal fashion. "Conserve your strength."

"No – Kate," he persisted, "it is of the utmost importance. My conscience must be cleared this very night, if only for selfish reasons."

Her heart sank. What could he mean? His conscience? Selfish reasons? What could plague his thoughts so unless... Her mind ran amok. Was it possible Edwin had become attached to someone more worthy? Was his haste to reach Longlea necessitated by the request for a divorce? The mere supposition shattered her being.

"I have been less than a husband to you for many weeks now," Edwin continued quietly. "When you had need of my support I failed to give it. Indeed, God forgive me, I turned my back on you and stayed away." Pain etched its way over his swollen, bruised features and a look of despair pervaded his grey eyes.

At that moment he looked so vulnerable Kate wanted to throw herself into his arms and feel the gentleness of his caress, but alas, each word he spoke confirmed her worst fears and she could not in case of a rebuff. Her spirits were low. "I hold no bitterness toward you Edwin. Alas, to my everlasting shame, it was I who wronged you," she stated dejectedly.

"The wrong or right of it is now unimportant," he chided softly. "All that matters is your forgiveness and the future."

"I understand," Kate nodded her head in acceptance. "I will release you from our vows, of course," she concluded, resigning herself to the inevitable.

Edwin stared at her with a puzzled expression. "Release me? But why, I do not…"

"You have met someone else, have you not?" Kate interrupted. " And now you wish for a divorce," she concluded, gazing into his eyes and speaking with the directness he had always admired.

"Divorce?" Edwin, aghast and overcome by her words, momentarily forgot his injuries in reaching for her. "My dearest Kate, no such notion has ever entered my mind. I merely wanted, no desperately needed your forgiveness."

Kate was confused. "But your haste to reach Longlea?"

He raised her hand to his bruised lips then squeezed it reassuringly. "Would you be so kind as to fetch my overcoat, the one I was wearing earlier."

Upon her return to the couch, Edwin extracted with difficulty, an envelope from his inside pocket and passed it over to her. "Well open it Kate and tell me, what do you see?"

Slowly Kate took out the card. To her surprise she found a colourful invitation to a celebratory meal for Mr and Mrs Edwin Jameson at Monsieur Jacques in Hislop Lane on the eighth of November and confirmation of a booking at the Royal the following two days.

The curiosity of it all overwhelmed her. "But..." she began.

"Have you noted the date my dear? The eighth is our wedding anniversary is it not?" he whispered softly. "And since a visit to Paris would be out of the question in these dangerous times, I thought perhaps a visit to Monsieur Jacques restaurant would help us in some small way to recapture a little French atmosphere."

Kate could hardly contain her relief and as she knelt at his side, the softness of her deep brown eyes brimmed with tears of joy.

"I do not deserve such happiness," she concluded weakly.

"Please," he begged, "can you find it in your heart to begin life afresh with an obstinate fool such as I?"

"Edwin, you are all things to me. My life has purpose but no direction without you," she confirmed simply.

"Then this evening I am doubly blessed," he reiterated with a smile of satisfaction.

"I must telephone the Royal Hotel and Monsieur Jacques later this afternoon to inform them of your unfortunate accident and that we must postpone the bookings until you have fully recovered," Kate remarked.

"Perhaps this year we can celebrate the occasion more quietly at home."

Edwin's pleasure was obvious.

"And," Kate added smugly, rising to her feet, "as it is my responsibility to sustain your well-being, I must insist that you rest now."

Despite the discomfort of his injuries a mischievous twinkle entered Edwin's eyes.

"Ah," he sighed, "would the nurses at the County Hospital have bullied me in such a fashion I wonder?"

"No," Kate replied joyously, leaning forward to place a kiss upon his bruised forehead, "for none would have loved you as I do."

"That is, I believe, sufficient reason for me to submit," he conceded happily as he lowered his body beneath the blankets and closed his eyes.

About the Author

I was born in Northamptonshire and love the County. The villages, with their eye-catching cottages are a special blend of Englishness and days gone by and strolling through them whatever the season offers a kind of stability. Yet the area is less than seventy odd miles away from the City of London and approximately eighty-five miles from the nearest seaside resort. This has to be a bonus. A County set twixt sea and sand and galleries and museums.

Apart from being devoted to my ever-expanding family, I have numerous hobbies, incorporating all kinds of reading material and a truly wide range of music. In addition, I play the piano and organ purely for my own enjoyment.

My true pleasure however lies in writing. Creating characters and breathing life into them on paper. Sometimes words spill out on to the page and other times I'm frustrated for hours by that one elusive phrase that reveals something special about a character. But when it finally comes together the experience is magical.

Over the years, I have written short stories and numerous pieces of poetry that have been published in various magazines, including a book of poetry published by Nene Arts. This however, is my first foray into writing a romantic novel. Another book of a different genre is almost ready, with the germ of another all set to fill the gap.

Con
44 858 30924

Pin 2573 .

Sat / Sun
224407

£259 20 .

Lightning Source UK Ltd.
Milton Keynes UK
UKOW05f1534230617
303960UK00001B/7/P

9 781786 238702